Double Dog Date Ya

by Stephanie Green

Double Dog Date Ya

© 2025 Stephanie Green

Published by Forged in Fire Studios

Texarkana, Texas

www.ForgedInFireStudios.com

Cover design by Stephanie Green

Interior layout by Stephanie Green

First Edition, 2025

ISBN: 9798271910388

Printed in the United States of America

For Jamie, Jaylen, Ava, and CJ—

my favorite love story.

Thank you for believing in every comeback,

and for reminding me that even the messiest moments

can lead us home.

Chapter 1 – Nate

I wake to the sound of someone screaming and the familiar, low growl of my father's old dog.

Light slams through the curtains. My head's pounding, my chest's tight, and there's a woman standing at the foot of my bed, screaming, clutching her purse like she's about to fight off a ghost.

"Are you OD'ing? Oh my God—are you OD'ing?"

My tongue feels like sandpaper, my vision's going gray around the edges. I fumble on the nightstand, knock over a glass of water, and find the orange bottle of glucose tablets instead of anything illicit. I can't form words yet, just point at the label while Diesel, my late father's German Shepherd, lifts his head and sighs.

"Not—drugs," I manage to croak. "Low sugar."

She stares, wild-eyed. "I'm not going to jail because you died!"

Before I can explain that I'm diabetic, not contagious, she bolts for the door, heels in hand.

"It's not contagious!" I yell after her.

The door slams. I add under my breath, "Hope you weren't."

Diesel lets out another deep, judgmental exhale.

"Don't look at me like that," I tell him, chewing two chalky tablets. "You're just as codependent as she was."

The sugar rushes back in slow waves. My hands stop shaking. I lie there a second, staring at the ceiling fan that wobbles like it's had too much champagne. There's an empty bottle of the real stuff on the nightstand, half a tuxedo shirt on the floor, and a single earring in my shoe.

Another great morning in the Callahan penthouse.

I reach down and scratch Diesel's ear. "You'd tell me if I was turning into him, right?"

He just yawns, heavy and patient—the same look my dad used to get when I'd screw up, which is fitting since Diesel was my dad's partner. I inherited him, along with the condo and the guilt.

Diesel's coat is silvered now, thick and coarse along the shoulders, darker down the spine like smoke still clinging to steel. One ear notches slightly at the tip from an old bite. His muzzle's gone salt-and-pepper, eyes deep amber and too knowing—like he's seen everything bad a man can do and still decided to stay.

I glance at the glucose monitor blinking on the nightstand. 58. Not terrible. Not great either.

The silence presses in, thick and humming. Somewhere between the expensive silence of success and the kind of quiet that sounds like punishment.

"Ahh," I say, voice rough. "Fuckin' diabetes."

Diesel's tail thumps once. Slow approval—or pity.

"Thanks for the vote of confidence, D."

I sigh. "Who am I kidding? You're basically my dad reincarnated, aren't you?"

I swing my legs off the bed, feet hitting the cold marble, and try to ignore the way the room tilts. Another day, another hangover I can't afford and a dog that still looks at me like I might someday be worth saving.

Diesel's already trotting toward the living room before I can stand. That's never a good sign.

"Hey, hero—what did we destroy today?"

No answer, obviously. Just the click of claws on marble and the ominous sound of something soft being shredded.

I follow the trail: tie, sock, piece of my sanity. The living room looks like a department-store crime scene. My favorite couch—Italian leather, or what's left of it—has been "customized." There's stuffing everywhere, white tufts floating through a shaft of morning light like snow. Diesel sits in the middle of it, chest out, tail sweeping lazily, a single strip of leather hanging from his mouth.

"Fantastic," I mutter. "You're really embracing retirement."

He drops the evidence on my rug and looks proud.

"Let me guess—low blood sugar again? You can smell it on me now too, can't you?"

He blinks once. I swear this dog understands full sentences.

I pick up my phone from the coffee table—thirteen missed calls from unknown numbers, one from my broker, and one text from Ziggy, the dog trainer my father swore by.

ZIGGY: Diesel's check-in overdue. Don't make me send karma your way.

Ziggy Daug. Cousin to every stray dog and half the city's spiritual weirdos.

I groan. "Right. Vet day. Check-in. Obedience refresher. Because clearly I'm the one who needs training."

I shuffle to the kitchen, step over a ripped pillow, and open the fridge. It's a graveyard of take-out boxes and a single vial of insulin staring back at me like a tiny, glass conscience. I tap the pen, sigh, and shoot up while Diesel watches.

"You'd think after all these years I'd get used to it," I tell him. "But nope. Every time, still feels like my old man's ghost is laughing."

The shot burns; I don't flinch.

Dad had it too—same disease, same stubborn streak. Drank himself through it until it killed him. I like to think I'm different, but the champagne bottle in the sink disagrees.

Diesel noses my hand, and for a second I let him. His fur's rough against my palm, grounding. Then the moment passes; I pull away.

"Okay, partner. Let's go pay our karmic debt to the dog-whispering hippie."

I grab my keys, step into yesterday's jeans, and follow Diesel to the elevator. The mirrored walls reflect a man who looks fine on paper: sharp jaw, expensive watch, no reason in the world to be miserable.

But the eyes? They tell the truth.

When the doors open on the lobby, Diesel lunges forward, tail high, ready for whatever's next.

I wish I could say the same.

Chapter 2 – Nate

By the time I pull up to Namaste & Fetch, the city is already too awake for me.

The storefront is all glass and optimism—plants spilling from planters, a chalkboard sign out front that reads:

Puppy Yoga Today – Find Your Balance & Your Best Friend!

"Find my best friend," I tell Diesel. "Guess that means you've been demoted."

He pants happily, fogging up the glass as we step inside.

The smell hits first: lavender, dog treats, and something herbal that could double as air freshener or witchcraft. Acoustic guitar hums softly—too serene for the anxiety bubbling in my chest.

Then I see her.

A woman with copper-brown hair tied in a messy knot kneels beside a basket of chew toys, wearing leggings patterned with tiny suns. Light catches the loose strands framing her face, turning them into filaments of gold. She looks calm in a way I forgot people could look.

She wipes her hands and freezes like I've just walked into a sacred ritual.

"Uh—hi," I say, adjusting Diesel's leash. "I'm here for… whatever this is."

Her eyes travel from my shoes to my face, unimpressed. "This is a puppy-yoga fundraiser. You're late."

"Story of my life."

She doesn't smile. "You brought a police dog to puppy yoga?"

"He's retired."

"Does he like other dogs?"

"He tolerates me, so probably not."

The corners of her mouth twitch. "Perfect."

She stands—graceful, steady, the kind of calm that makes me suddenly aware of every bad habit I've ever had. "I'm Sienna," she says. "Owner, instructor, referee."

"Nate."

"Callahan?"

I blink. "That obvious?"

"The badge tag on his collar." She gestures to Diesel. "Patrick Callahan's dog. I used to see them at the park when I was a kid."

Of course she did. The universe really loves its callbacks.

Before I can come up with something clever, she claps her hands and calls to the room, "All right, everyone—find your mats and your breath!"

The music swells. Twelve people in matching stretchy hope pants drop into downward dog while a parade of puppies sniffs their hair, chews their shoelaces, and performs unsanctioned acts of rebellion. A golden retriever puppy climbs onto someone's back mid-pose; a dachshund is attempting theft by yoga block.

Sienna moves through them effortlessly—barefoot, calm, voice low and melodic. "Inhale… exhale… let the dogs remind you how to live in the moment."

Diesel sits beside me, watching the madness with the same expression I'm wearing: horror with a side of disbelief.

"I told you," I whisper, "we're in a cult."

Then she bends to adjust a mat, sunlight skimming her shoulders, and for one inconvenient second I forget how to breathe. Her focus, the quiet authority—it's magnetic in the way a thunderstorm is.

That's when Diesel decides serenity is overrated.

He locks on a French bulldog in a sweater and growls low. The bulldog barks back.

Within seconds, half a dozen dogs are losing their minds— mats turning into trampolines, zen instantly dying.

Sienna dives into the fray like a firefighter. "Everyone stay calm!" she calls, but the words drown under a chorus of barks.

Diesel jerks his leash from my hand and charges. I lunge after him, slip on a mat, and crash spectacularly onto my back.

Somewhere in the chaos, fabric rips.

The room goes silent.

Sienna's standing over me, one eyebrow raised, trying not to smile.

I glance down. Yep. Pants: deceased.

She exhales through her nose, equal parts patience and disbelief. "You okay?"

"Define okay."

Behind her, Diesel has stolen a squeaky toy and declared victory.

"Your dog," she says, "might be the most disruptive force I've ever met."

"Yeah," I grunt, standing and trying to salvage my dignity. "Runs in the family."

A voice from the back calls out, "Told you, Lennon! The universe never sends boring men—just ones that need extra yoga!"

A bald man in a turquoise shirt emerges, waving incense like a victory flag.

"Ziggy Daug," he announces, bowing. "Spiritual director, treat distributor, resident chaos translator."

He points at me. "You're vibrating at a 'fix me' frequency, my dude. Luckily, we're open-minded."

Sienna groans. "Ziggy, not now."

"Especially now," he says, smiling. "Because this—" he gestures between me and Sienna "—has potential. Dogs are the universe's matchmakers."

I blink. "Pretty sure mine just tried to murder a Frenchie."

Ziggy shrugs. "Love is messy."

Sienna closes her eyes like she's praying for patience.

I'm starting to think she might need it—because for the first time in a long time, I'm tempted to stick around and see what happens next.

Chapter 3 – Sienna

The smell of lavender and wet dog clings to my hair long after the last yoga mat is rolled up. Ziggy hums somewhere behind me, reorganizing crystal bowls that don't need reorganizing. Diesel's toy—a squeaky giraffe—lies headless near the door, its white fluff scattered like snow after a storm. The only part that still makes it recognizable is the neck. Figures. I scoop it up gently, the silence after its squeak somehow louder than the class itself.

"Hey, Lennon," Ziggy calls—he's the only person who ever uses my middle name. Sometimes it sounds like a jab at my parents' hippie streak, sometimes it's the closest he gets to I love you. "You okay, or are we about to add deep breathing to the list of required safety protocols?"

"I'm fine," I say. Always the first lie of the day.

He pokes his head around the curtain, incense smoke curling over his shoulder like a lazy ghost. Ziggy looks like someone the universe made during a glitter shortage—then overcompensated for. His linen shirt is open halfway down his chest, layered necklaces tangled with a pendant shaped like a crescent moon. His jeans shimmer faintly when he moves, like they've been dusted with starlight or possibly actual glitter. His silver nail polish is chipped, his eyeliner perfect.

He's the kind of person who somehow makes chaos look curated, like if enlightenment had a sequined PR manager.

"That guy was… something," he says, tilting his head. "Kind of hot in a haunted-house way."

I shoot him a look. "He brought a police dog to a puppy class, Ziggy."

"Every love story starts with a bad decision."

I groan. "You're impossible."

"I'm enlightened." He winks and starts stacking mats with the exaggerated grace of someone performing for invisible cameras. "Tell me I'm wrong."

I don't. Because he's not, exactly.

Nate Callahan looked like every red flag I swore I'd stop collecting—expensive watch, defensive smile, eyes that hide everything. The kind of man who uses charm like armor. Broad shoulders under a faded T-shirt, jaw shadowed with exhaustion, hands that looked like they used to build things before life convinced them to break instead. He moved like someone used to control but not peace.

The kind of man my mother would have fallen for.

That thought drags a shiver through me, fast and uninvited.

The fluorescent light flickers once. Suddenly I'm back in that hospital hallway—the smell of disinfectant, the metallic taste of fear. A nurse shouting for crash carts, a stretcher flying past me.

My mother's voice, weak but urgent: "Don't let them take Monroe to jail."

The memory snaps shut as quickly as it came. Ziggy's hand lands lightly on my shoulder. His rings are always cold.

"Hey," he says softly. "You went somewhere."

"Just… tired."

He studies me for a beat but lets it go. "You want me to handle the rescue check-in tomorrow? Give you a day?"

"No. I'll be fine."

He grins. "Translation: you'll work through your feelings by alphabetizing dog toys again."

"Exactly."

He starts toward the door, then turns back. His bracelets jingle like wind chimes. "He's coming back, you know."

"Who?"

"Nate Callahan. I felt it in the air. Karma, attraction, or maybe I just smelled his cologne—it's still here, by the way."

He leaves before I can answer. The door jingles shut behind him.

I sink onto the mat and stare at the tiny patch of sunlight creeping across the floor. Diesel's chew toy squeaks under my foot.

"Don't let them take him to jail," my mother's voice whispers again, faint and old.

I press my palms together, close my eyes, and breathe until all I can smell is lavender again. For a moment more I linger on the thought that he'd be back soon. Then, I quietly mumble to myself: "Girl, don't do it. You're allergic to red flags and still keep petting them."

The room stays silent, like it already knows I'm lying.

Chapter 4 – Nate

If hell had a waiting room, it would smell like motor oil and wet fur. That's my first thought when I pull into the cracked-asphalt lot of The Yard, Ziggy Daug's idea of a "training facility." The sign out front hangs crooked, hand-painted in teal:

THE YARD – Behavior Rehabilitation & Other Miracles.

Diesel sniffs the air, tail twitching like he's clocked in for duty. "Don't get your hopes up," I tell him. "We're here because you ate half my couch, not because I believe in miracles."

A chain-link gate groans open, and a man steps out—tall, tan, shoulders broad enough to cast shade, long hair tied back in a loose man bun that somehow doesn't look pretentious on him. His T-shirt clings to a torso carved from real labor, not gym mirrors; his forearms are roped with muscle and peppered with pale scars that say he's met teeth before. There's a calm steadiness in how he moves, like the ground adjusts to him, not the other way around.

He's tossing a tennis ball to a Rottweiler who moves like an old prizefighter—slow, deliberate, lethal if provoked. Dust rises in lazy clouds around their boots and paws; the whole place smells like sun-baked rubber, leather, and loyalty.

"You Callahan?" he calls.

"Guilty."

He wipes his hands on his jeans. "Jax Rivers."

Figures. The name alone sounds like it should come with a guitar solo.

He gestures toward Diesel. "Heard this one's a handful."

"Define handful."

"The kind that eats furniture and hierarchy."

He crouches, letting Diesel sniff his palm. Up close, I see the small burn marks along his knuckles and the easy patience in his expression—the kind of confidence that doesn't need to announce itself.

"Smart dog," he says. "Too much time with an owner who doesn't know what to do with loyalty."

I bristle. "You read all that from one sniff?"

"Dogs don't lie, man."

He rises, meeting my eyes—steady, unflinching. "You do."

Diesel sits beside him, the traitor.

Jax whistles, and a half-dozen dogs appear from behind a fence—mutts, shepherds, pits, one shaggy husky with a scar over its eye. The Rottweiler limps to his side, tail wagging once. "Tank," Jax says. "Retired like your boy. Difference is, Tank listens."

Tank's muzzle is gray, his stance pure authority—one of those dogs that doesn't bark because he never needs to. He fixes Diesel with a slow blink that says respect your elders, and Diesel actually does.

I cross my arms. "So what's the magic trick? Chanting? Sage? Ziggy already burned enough of that stuff to summon ghosts."

Jax smirks. "Nah. Just patience. You got any?"

"Depends on the day."

He nods toward a battered obstacle course—tires, ramps, old barrels, everything sun-bleached and chewed at the edges. "Then today's not your day."

He sets Diesel loose with the others. My stomach tightens. For a second, Diesel stands rigid, assessing. Then he charges—straight through the middle of the pack, scattering them like bowling pins. Tank gives a single warning bark; Diesel freezes, surprised.

Jax whistles again, low and sharp. Every dog except Diesel sits instantly. Diesel looks at me, waiting for my cue. I have none.

"Tell him to sit," Jax says.

I clear my throat. "Sit."

Diesel cocks his head. Nothing.

"Use your body," Jax says. "He's reading you, not the word."

I exhale, square my shoulders, point down. "Sit."

This time Diesel lowers his haunches, eyes locked on me. A flicker of pride slips through the irritation.

Jax nods once. "See? He wants to follow you. You just keep leading him into traffic."

"Touché."

Jax's grin is quick and genuine, sunlight catching on a tiny scar at the corner of his mouth. "You free tomorrow? We run drills at dawn."

I glance at my shoes—wrong color for dirt. "I'm more of a noon person."

"Dawn," he repeats. "That's when the noise in your head's quiet enough for him to hear you."

He walks off, Tank limping at his heel, leaving me standing in the middle of The Yard—heat shimmering off metal fences, dogs settling into the hum of obedience—Diesel at my side, both of us trying to figure out what just happened.

Diesel nudges my hand with his nose. "Yeah," I mutter. "I didn't expect to like him either."

But when my alarm goes off at 5 a.m., I already know I'm getting up.

Chapter 5 – Sienna

The rescue always smells like hope covered in bleach.

Cages line the converted warehouse, each with a face staring out—some eager, some resigned. The sound is a strange harmony: paws against metal, a dozen different kinds of breathing. It's both heartbreak and peace.

"Mooorning, Lennonnn," Lila calls from the back, stretching out my middle name with a grin. She knows I only let Ziggy get away with it, which is exactly why she does it. It's her way of saying, I see you, and I'm going to make you laugh whether you like it or not.

She's balancing two bowls of kibble and wearing a sweatshirt that says My Therapist Has Fur.

Lila Rivers is built of soft strength—part saint, part overworked single mom—and somehow still manages to smell like cinnamon rolls and dog shampoo. Her dark hair is twisted into a messy braid that keeps slipping loose, strands framing a face that's both tired and radiant. There's a streak of silver at her temple that she refuses to dye, freckles dusting her nose, and the same sun-warmed tan as her brother—though where Jax's intensity feels like wildfire, Lila's glows steady, like candlelight. Her eyes are a deep, steady brown, the kind that make people confess things they didn't mean to.

"Morning," I answer, ducking into the office where she's just finished a stack of adoption paperwork.

"You look exhausted," she says. "That means the class was either a success or a spiritual disaster."

"Somewhere between," I tell her. "A Frenchie almost met its maker, a man ripped his pants, and Ziggy declared it a sign from the universe."

Lila laughs. "So… normal Tuesday?"

"Pretty much."

She pushes a coffee toward me—the cheap kind that somehow tastes like comfort. "You're gonna burn yourself out, you know."

"I've been burnt," I say lightly. "Now I'm just aromatherapy."

Lila smirks. "You should come by on Saturday. We're short on volunteers."

"I'll be there. How's Tank doing?"

Her smile dims a little. "Still stiff, but Jax says he's getting stronger."

The mention of her brother always makes me straighten, as if the air around him demands posture. "He still running that miracle yard of his?"

"Every day at sunrise." She tilts her head. "You'd like him if you gave him a chance."

"I don't have time to like anyone right now."

"That's your problem, Lennon. You never think you have time for good things."

She says it so gently it lands more like truth than criticism. Before I can answer, she waves a folder. "Speaking of good things, I've got a fundraising nightmare for you."

"Oh no."

"Oh yes. The city pulled our grant again. I need something flashy. Something people talk about."

"Flashy?" I repeat, already regretting asking.

She grins. "You and Ziggy are good at weird. Make it work for us."

Later, driving home, her words loop in my head. Something flashy. Something weird. I pass the park where the puppy-yoga fiasco took place; a couple of strangers are laughing over coffee while their dogs tumble in the grass.

Flashy. Weird. Joyful. The kind of thing that makes people feel good enough to open their wallets.

And then the thought hits—ridiculous, obvious, perfect. What if the dogs chose the dates?

A charity dating event where the dogs decided who got a second chance.

I laugh out loud at the absurdity of it—and at how good it feels to imagine something fun for once.

By the time I reach the studio, I've already texted Ziggy:

ME: Got an idea.

ZIGGY: Does it involve glitter or enlightenment?

ME: Both. And dogs. Lots of dogs.

Chapter 6 – Nate

Sunrise is for farmers, saints, and people who hate themselves.

I am none of those things.

Diesel sits at my feet, alert, as Jax Rivers circles us with a coffee mug the size of a trophy. The air smells like dirt, dew, and punishment. The grass is still wet enough to soak through my shoes.

"Rule number one," Jax says. "You're not the boss of him if you're not the boss of you."

"I didn't sign up for therapy."

He smirks. "You did. You just don't remember filling out the form."

He tosses a leash toward me. I fumble it like a rookie.

Diesel stays perfectly still, eyes locked on Jax. The traitor again.

"Walk him," Jax says.

"We're walking."

"No," he says, "you're dragging."

We circle the fenced yard. Diesel tugs ahead; I tug back. A small dog yaps from behind a crate, and Diesel freezes, muscles tightening. The leash pulls tight enough to sting my hand. He's waiting for orders I don't know how to give.

"Talk to him," Jax calls.

"I am."

"Not like that. Mean it."

I sigh. "Diesel, sit."

Diesel looks at me, then sits. The obedience feels like luck more than skill, but Jax nods as if I've just solved an equation.

"See?" he says. "He doesn't need you to be perfect. Just present."

"That's poetic. You knit that on pillows too?"

Jax grins. "No, man. I just work with people who forget they're animals too."

I open my mouth to reply when the gate screeches open and Ziggy's voice breaks the thin morning calm like a cymbal crash.

"Good morning, miracle workers!"

He's wearing tie-dye, sunglasses, and carrying two lattes.

Jax groans. "You're early."

"I'm vibrating at a sunrise frequency," Ziggy says. "Also, the universe told me to bring caffeine."

He hands me a cup. "You look like someone whose soul needs stretching."

"I'm good."

"Liar," he says cheerfully, and plops down on a hay bale like he owns the place. "So this is where the magic happens? Smells like redemption—and manure."

"Mostly manure," I mutter.

Jax throws Diesel a treat. "Your boy's a fast learner."

"Must've inherited my dad's instincts," I say, half proud, half bitter.

Ziggy sips his coffee. "You talk about your dad like he's both a saint and a ghost. Which is it?"

"Depends on the day."

"Maybe it's both," he says. "Even ghosts can teach you things if you stop running."

I glance at him. "You always this deep before breakfast?"

He grins. "Always."

Jax claps his hands. "Alright, philosopher, let's put you to use. Grab a leash. You're spotting today."

Ziggy stands, delighted. "The universe provides! Which one's mine?"

I shake my head, watching as Jax hands him a leash attached to a nervous golden mix. Ziggy whispers something to the dog and immediately gets a lick across the face.

"See?" Ziggy beams. "Instant chemistry."

Diesel snorts. I swear it's laughter.

For the first time in a long time, I catch myself smiling—an actual, unforced smile—and it feels strange. Foreign.

Jax notices but says nothing.

Ziggy does. Of course he does.

"There it is," he says softly. "Proof of life."

Chapter 7 – Sienna

The first rule of fundraising: never brainstorm with Ziggy before caffeine.

The second rule: ignore rule one if you want lightning in a bottle.

He's already in the studio when I arrive, barefoot, hair tied up in a scarf that looks like it's hiding illegal fireworks. The scent of espresso, sage, and something faintly citrus hums through the room.

"You're early," I say, locking the door behind me.

"I'm vibrating with destiny," he replies. "Also oat milk."

"Morning, Leeeennnooon," he adds, stretching my middle name like he's testing how far he can push me.

"Trying to start the day on a positive note, Dawgy," I say, giving him a side-eye for using Lennon.

He grins, unbothered. "Always."

I drop my bag on the counter. "We need an idea. Lila's grant fell through again."

"I know," he says, eyes sparkling. "The universe woke me at three a.m. whispering love and dogs."

"I had the same whisper, minus the hallucination part." I pour coffee into a chipped mug. "Ready?"

Ziggy sits cross-legged on the floor. "Lay it on me, Lennon."

I pace. "A dating fundraiser. We call it—wait for it—Double Dog Date Ya. Like the dare. Double dog dare ya. Singles bring their dogs. The dogs decide who gets a second date."

He gasps like I've handed him enlightenment in a mason jar. "That's—Lennon—that's karmic genius."

"I was thinking more like organized chaos."

"Exactly! Controlled spontaneity. Love guided by wet noses." He claps his hands. "We can use the park by the rescue, bring in vendors, the pup-cake truck—"

"Food truck couple would love that," I say. "They'll bake until dawn if it's for a good cause."

Ziggy's pacing now. "We'll livestream it! Sponsors! Local press! We'll call it Love at First Bark!"

"Please don't," I groan, but he's unstoppable.

"You host. Obviously."

"No way."

"Yes way. You're the calm in the storm. People trust calm."

"They trust you. You could sell enlightenment door-to-door."

"Lennon." He stops pacing. "You need this."

I blink. "I need a nap."

"You need to remember joy isn't a luxury. It's a survival tactic."

The words hit harder than I expect. Joy and survival. Two things I used to think couldn't exist in the same sentence.

He sees my silence and softens. "Look, you've spent years helping everyone else heal. Maybe this helps you too."

I stare out the window at a couple walking their dog through the morning fog, the leash looping between them like connection made visible. A laugh catches halfway in my throat, more breath than sound.

"Fine," I say with a sharp exhale—trying not to smile. "But you handle the press."

He grins. "Deal. Now tell me we can have matching shirts."

"Only if they don't have glitter."

"No promises."

That night I stay late after class, sketching layout plans in a notebook that still smells faintly of lavender. Every line I draw feels lighter than the last. For the first time in months, I'm not replaying the hospital hallway or the sound of my mother's voice.

Just dogs, laughter, and maybe—just maybe—a little hope.

Chapter 8 – Nate

Diesel's snoring like a freight train.

Sunlight cuts across the kitchen counter, catching the steam from my second cup of coffee as I scroll emails that all start with urgent and end with investment opportunity. My phone buzzes with the kind of text that can only come from Ziggy Daug.

ZIGGY: Congrats, you're a contestant!

ME: On what?

ZIGGY: Love.

ME: I'll pass.

ZIGGY: Too late. I double-dog dared ya.

I stare at the screen. "Double dog… what?"

Diesel thumps his tail once, the universal sign for you're doomed.

A second later, the phone rings.

"Nate Callahan," I answer, voice flat.

Ziggy's voice bursts through like a parade. "My man! The universe has chosen you for greatness—and maybe emotional stability. How's your calendar next Saturday?"

"I don't do weekends," I say. "Or greatness."

"You'll make an exception for Double Dog Date Ya."

"Sounds like a cult."

"It's a fundraiser."

"For what?"

"Love, charity, and possibly rabies shots. Don't overthink it."

"I'm hanging up now."

"You can't! Lila already printed your name on the flyer. And your dog's."

I glance at Diesel, who's now chewing the corner of my shoe like he knows he's complicit.

"You used my dog's name?"

"Marketing, man. He's photogenic. You're the grumpy one people root for."

I rub my temples. "You forged my signature, didn't you?"

"I prefer to call it energetic manifestation."

I sigh. "Ziggy—"

He cuts me off. "Look, you owe me for that obedience miracle Jax pulled off last week. Come on, it's one day. You bring Diesel, pretend to mingle, look handsome for the cause. There'll be food trucks. Pup-cakes. Maybe a journalist or two."

"I'm allergic to both journalists and mingling."

"Perfect! You'll stand out."

Before I can argue, he hangs up.

Diesel stares at me, tail still sweeping the floor.

"You're enjoying this," I say.

He yawns.

I scroll through my messages again and spot a link Ziggy sent. The event flyer flashes across my screen:

DOUBLE DOG DATE YA!

A charity matchmaking event for animal rescue and
hopeless romantics.

Underneath: a photo of Ziggy holding two puppies like
trophies and—God help me—a candid shot of me at The
Yard with Diesel, both of us looking mildly competent.

They must've taken it when I wasn't looking.

That afternoon, I show up at The Yard to demand answers.
Jax is tossing a ball to Tank when I stomp in.

"Morning, Wall Street," he says without turning.

"You know about this?"

He smirks. "Ziggy told me to save the date."

"I'm not doing a dog-dating carnival."

He shrugs. "Could be worse. Could be therapy."

"This is therapy."

He chuckles, tossing the ball again. "You might surprise yourself. People show up for the dogs. They stay for the second chances."

I want to argue, but Diesel's already rolling in the dirt with Tank like a toddler at recess.

"Traitor," I mutter.

Jax claps my shoulder. "See you Saturday."

Saturday. Love. Second chances.

Sounds like the setup to a bad joke—and I'm the punchline.

I'm secretly hoping the animals are the only "dogs" doing the dating.

But here I am, already trying to find pants that won't split in public.

Chapter 9 – Sienna

If organization were a sport, I'd have a gold medal and matching yoga mat.

Too bad chaos never read a spreadsheet.

By ten a.m., the studio looks like a carnival collided with a rescue center. Boxes of banners, donation jars, and dog treats tower in uneven stacks. Lila's perched on a stool, her laptop balanced on one knee; Ziggy's sitting cross-legged on the counter, eating cereal out of a mixing bowl.

"Okay," I say, clapping my hands. "Let's review. Vendors confirmed?"

Lila checks her list. "Food-truck couple's in. They're bringing pup-cakes, bark-scotti, and something called the Pupperoni Dream Sandwich."

"Perfect."

Ziggy raises his spoon. "If they need a taste tester, the universe has blessed me with a resilient digestive system."

I give him a look. "The last time you said that, you hallucinated a raccoon spirit guide."

"That raccoon had wisdom."

"His name was Trashbag, Ziggy."

"Still wise."

Lila hides her laugh behind her coffee cup. "Okay, Lennon, what about contestants?"

"Ziggy's handling sign-ups," I say, already regretting it.

"Delegation!" he chirps. "That's leadership."

I pull up the online registration form on my tablet. "So far, we've got twenty-four singles confirmed, plus a waiting list."

"Any familiar faces?" Lila asks.

"Some of my yoga clients, a few rescue volunteers, and …" My eyes narrow. "Wait — Nate Callahan?"

Ziggy freezes mid-bite. "Surprise?"

"Surprise?" I repeat. "You signed up the guy whose dog nearly destroyed my class?"

"He needed a push — the man's heart chakra is basically under quarantine."

"Ziggy!"

"What? He's perfect! He's grumpy, handsome, emotionally constipated — it's charity catnip!"

Lila snorts. "He's not wrong."

I fold my arms. "You can't just enter people into a dating event."

He grins. "I double-dog dared him."

"You what?"

"It's the brand, Lennon! Double Dog Date Ya! I'm just living the message."

I press my fingers to my temples. "This is going to be a disaster."

"Or destiny," he counters, twirling his spoon. "Same number of letters."

Lila leans over my shoulder to peek at the list. "You should at least admit he's good for publicity. That photo of him and Diesel? Instant clickbait."

I sigh. "Fine. But if he starts another canine riot, you're both cleaning it up."

Ziggy salutes with his cereal spoon. "Yes, ma'am. I'll even bring sage."

Later that night, I spread the event flyers across my kitchen table — each one louder, brighter, bolder than the last.

Ziggy's tagline glares up at me in cheerful font:

Find love. Or at least a leash partner.

I trace the outline of the logo with my finger, trying not to think about Nate Callahan's face on the promotional banner.

Grumpy, handsome, emotionally constipated.

Ziggy wasn't wrong.

I shake my head, laughing under my breath. "It's just a fundraiser," I remind myself.

But somewhere deep in my chest, something feels like a dare.

Chapter 10 – Nate

I knew this was a mistake before I even parked.

The city park's been transformed into a dog-themed carnival—bunting strung between trees, picnic tables draped in paw-print cloths, vendors handing out pup-cakes with names like Chews Wisely and Fur Real Love. A banner stretches above the small stage in unapologetic neon pink:

DOUBLE DOG DATE YA!

Find love. Or at least a leash partner.

I immediately start scanning for the nearest exit.

Diesel, however, is vibrating with joy—tail a metronome of betrayal.

"Don't get too excited," I tell him. "We're here for ten minutes. We pose, we donate, we leave."

He ignores me, already greeting a golden retriever like they survived a war together.

Ziggy appears out of thin air wearing a sequined vest and a headset mic. "Ladies, gentlemen, and magnificent emotional-support beings!" he bellows, arms wide. "Welcome to Double Dog Date Ya!"

I pinch the bridge of my nose. "Oh God. He's amplified."

Ziggy spots me and lights up. "And there's our reluctant leading man! Give it up for Nate Callahan and the magnificent Diesel!"

A cheer ripples through the crowd. Diesel barks once— Oscar speech complete.

"Traitor," I mutter.

"Smile!" Ziggy yells, snapping a photo before I can dodge.

I turn toward the sign-in table—mostly to locate someone to blame—and there she is.

Sienna. Clipboard in hand. Sunlight catching the copper in her hair. She's wearing a pale-blue shirt knotted at the waist, radiating the kind of calm that looks effortless and probably costs her everything.

If I'm honest, she could wear dog hair over mud or mud over dog hair and still look composed.

She looks up, meets my eyes, and her smile freezes halfway.

"You've got to be kidding me," she says.

"Trust me," I reply. "If I were kidding, there'd be less glitter."

Ziggy slides between us like a referee. "Lennon! Surprise! Look what destiny dragged in."

"I see destiny brought a headache," she says.

"I didn't volunteer," I add.

"He was divinely coerced," Ziggy chirps. "And you two are—let me check my cosmic chart—paired for the first round!"

Her jaw drops. "You what?"

Diesel thumps his tail against my leg. He's definitely smiling.

Ziggy claps his hands. "Rules are simple! Each pair gets a picnic blanket, a basket, and fifteen minutes while your dogs interact. If both pups get along, you advance to round two—the Compatibility Leash Walk!"

Sienna presses her fingers to her temples. "This is chaos."

"Controlled chaos," Ziggy says proudly.

She looks at me like I'm a walking cautionary tale. "Fine. But keep him away from small dogs and baked goods."

"Noted," I say. "Though that eliminates most of the dating pool."

Her lips twitch despite herself. "Blanket number four," she mutters, leading the way.

Chapter 11 – Sienna

The park is still buzzing when the last whistle blows.

Laughter, barking, music, the hiss of the food-truck espresso machine—it all blends into one big heartbeat of noise.

Ziggy is on stage handing out ribbons shaped like tiny bones.

I'm trying to remember how breathing works.

"Good turnout," Lila says, sidling up beside me with a clipboard of donation totals. "And your grumpy Wall Street guy hasn't run for the hills yet."

"Give him time." I tug a stray leaf out of my hair. "He looks like he's surviving by sarcasm alone."

"Whatever works. People love him. He's brooding in a charming way." She nudges my arm. "You're blushing."

"I'm overheating," I insist. "Too much sun, too much chaos."

"Too much chemistry," she mutters, wandering off before I can argue.

I catch sight of Nate across the lawn—Diesel rolling in the grass at his feet while a group of kids fuss over him.

Nate's smiling. Not the quick, defensive grin from before. A real one.

It changes his whole face.

He looks… lighter.

I shake the thought away like a bug.

He must feel my eyes on him because he looks up, gives a small nod, and starts toward me.

Diesel trots beside him, tail high, carrying my clipboard in his mouth like an overachiever.

"Your assistant delivered this," Nate says, handing it over.

"Thanks."

He hesitates, then: "Can I ask you something?"

"Depends on the question."

"Why does Ziggy call you Lennon? Did I miss a memo?"

I laugh. "Middle name. My parents were musicians with a thing for symbolism. If I'm honest, I think my mom just got confused with Sierra Leone. Don't tell Ziggy. He'll start calling me Imagine."

"I'll take it to the grave," he says, then gives a small wave before Diesel drags him back toward the crowd.

Ziggy hops off the stage, headset askew, beaming like he's just solved world peace. "Lennon, my visionary! Did you see that turnout? The universe is howling with approval."

"I saw," I say, scanning the donation table. "We raised over a thousand in the first hour."

He gasps. "Abundance! Manifested through flirtation and fur."

"Through hard work and dog treats," I correct.

He ignores me, of course. "I'm telling you, Lennon, this event has legs—four of them, to be precise."

I roll my eyes. "I can't believe you paired me with Nate Callahan."

"Why not? Opposites attract. It's physics."

"It's lunacy."

"Tomato, tomahto."

Ziggy slips away to greet a group of reporters, leaving me with the sound of Diesel barking and Nate's voice somewhere in the crowd—low, amused, steady.

It shouldn't matter.

It doesn't matter.

Except that it does, and I hate that I know it.

By evening, the park has emptied. I sit on the tailgate of Lila's truck, flipping through photos on my phone: smiling couples, laughing dogs, a child hugging Diesel.

The light is gold, the kind that makes everything look kinder than it is.

"You did good, Lennon," Lila says softly, handing me a bottle of water. "You look happy."

"Don't start," I say, but I can't stop smiling.

"Whatever it is, let it happen," she says. "Life's too short to stay safe."

Her words echo, too close to my mother's voice, and for a second I'm back in that hospital hallway again—the panic, the stretcher, the plea I can never forget.

Don't let them take Monroe to jail.

I blink it away before the tears can start. "You heading home?"

"Yeah. You should too. You've got another round tomorrow."

I groan. "Don't remind me."

She laughs, climbing into her truck. "See you at dawn, hostess with the mostest."

When she drives off, I stay a minute longer, letting the quiet settle.

The park smells like grass and sugar and something softer I can't name.

Maybe hope.

Maybe trouble.

Probably both.

Chapter 12 – Nate

Diesel's been smiling all morning.

Yes, smiling — that smug, tongue-lolling grin of a dog who's discovered joy and refuses to let me forget it.

I, on the other hand, feel like I've been emotionally mugged.

The event was supposed to be one-and-done — a photo op, a check for charity, an exit.

Instead I left with grass stains, a mild sunburn, and a dog who's acting like he met his soulmate.

"Don't look at me like that," I mutter, pouring coffee. Morning light slants across the counter, catching the steam. "You had fun. I had public humiliation."

Diesel barks once, then noses the cabinet where I keep his treats.

"Oh, so now you're negotiating." I toss him one. "Fine. You win."

The treat vanishes in a single crunch.

I scroll through my phone and find that Ziggy has already posted a full recap to the event page: videos, photos, quotes, and — of course — a highlight reel titled Love Unleashed.

The thumbnail? Me and Sienna, mid-laugh, Diesel between us like some canine Cupid.

"Perfect," I say. "Immortalized in glitter and bad lighting."

A knock at the door interrupts my spiral.

When I open it, Jax stands there holding a paper bag that smells like coffee and judgment.

"Figured you'd need this," he says.

"I don't recall inviting you."

"You didn't." He walks in anyway, sets the bag on the counter. "Ziggy sent me to check on your spiritual hangover."

"I'm fine."

He studies me. "You've got that look."

"What look?"

"The one Tank gets when he's seen a squirrel he can't stop thinking about."

I groan. "You sound like Ziggy."

"Thanks."

Diesel trots over to Jax, tail wagging. The traitor.

Jax grins. "Looks like someone's got a crush."

"Yeah, on Sienna. He hasn't stopped grinning since she fed him a treat yesterday."

"Smart dog. She's a good one."

I raise an eyebrow. "You know her?"

"She volunteers at the rescue sometimes. My sister swears she's a saint."

"Great. Another reason to feel like an ass."

"Why's that?"

"Because saints don't usually get stuck babysitting sinners at dog fundraisers."

Jax laughs. "Relax, Callahan. You showed up. That's more than most people do."

He grabs his coffee, heading for the door. "Oh, by the way — Ziggy says you're officially in Round Two next weekend."

"What?"

"Something about public demand. Apparently the crowd loved you."

"Public demand?"

"Yup. People are rooting for the grumpy guy."

He leaves before I can argue.

Diesel hops onto the couch, lays his head on my knee, and sighs like he just finished saving the world.

"Don't get used to it," I tell him.

He thumps his tail once.

I scroll through the event photos one more time — Sienna laughing, sunlight in her hair, Diesel halfway in her lap.

Maybe Jax is right. Maybe showing up wasn't the worst thing I've done lately.

Still, I tell myself it doesn't mean anything.

It never does — right before it does.

Chapter 13 – Sienna

The morning after Double Dog Date Ya smells like coffee, disinfectant, and victory.

The rescue is a circus of wagging tails and exhaustion. Lila's counting cash donations at the desk, and Ziggy's perched on top of a crate like a tie-dyed gargoyle scrolling his phone.

"Three thousand, two hundred fourteen dollars," Lila announces, holding up the final tally. "Plus two checks from the food-truck couple."

I blink. "Wait—what? That's double our goal."

"Triple if you include karma points," Ziggy says without looking up. "Also, minor internet fame. Check this out."

He spins his phone toward me. My face—and Diesel's—fill the screen in a photo from yesterday. I'm mid-laugh, Diesel's licking my cheek, and right below it the caption reads:

#HotDogDad & the Zen Dog Whisperer

When opposites attract and adopt your heart.

I groan. "Please tell me you didn't post that."

"I didn't," Ziggy says. "The internet did. You're trending. The comments are unhinged."

Lila leans over his shoulder. "'That man can fetch my number anytime.' Oh my God—people are calling him Reluctant Romeo."

Ziggy beams. "It's art."

"It's a problem," I say, crossing my arms. "He's going to hate this."

"He already does," Ziggy replies cheerfully. "He called at six a.m. and said, 'Take it down before my broker sees it.' So I added a sparkle filter."

"Of course you did."

Every time someone says Nate Callahan, one of the dogs barks. I'm not even kidding. Lila's pit-mix lets out a low woof; the terrier joins in like gossip backup.

I glare at them. "Traitors."

Ziggy gasps theatrically. "See? Even the animals ship it!"

"Stop saying that word."

"Ship. Ship. Ship."

Lila's laughing so hard she nearly drops her clipboard. "He's right, though. You two were electric yesterday."

"Static," I correct. "Static shock. The painful kind."

Ziggy hops off the crate and stretches like a cat. "Whatever it was, the universe noticed. The comments want Round Two. Sponsors too. I already got an email from a leash company called Boundaries Be Gone."

I press my palms together. "I just wanted a simple fundraiser."

"And you created the Super Bowl of Love," Ziggy says proudly. "We're doing another round next weekend."

"Ziggy, no—"

"Yes, Lennon, yes. The rescue needs it. Lila, back me up."

Lila raises both hands. "Hey, I'm just the banker. But the money's real, and the dogs have never looked happier."

I look around. Every kennel tail is wagging. Even the shy shepherd who usually hides in the corner is standing by the gate, ears up, watching me.

Fine. Universe: 1. Me: 0.

Ziggy senses the surrender before I speak. "That's the face of consent," he says. "We're in!"

I point at him. "You handle the press."

He bows. "As always."

When the chaos settles, Lila and I box up the leftover treats. She hums softly, glowing in that post-event calm.

"You're thinking about him," she says.

"I'm thinking about invoices."

"Right. Invoices with cheekbones."

"Lila."

She laughs, leaning against a crate. "I'm serious, Sienna. It's okay to like someone. Even a complicated someone."

I pause, looking down at a red bandana left on the counter—Diesel's. Someone must have taken it off him before he left.

The fabric still smells like grass and something warm. I fold it carefully, pretending it's just laundry.

"I'm not saying I like him," I say.

"Of course you're not."

"I'm saying he's impossible."

"And impossible men make the best redemption stories," she says, heading for the door.

When she's gone, I stay a minute longer, turning the bandana over in my hands. It's ridiculous how something so small can hold so much noise.

Outside, the city hums—traffic, horns, life. Inside, the rescue dogs settle one by one, tails slowing to soft thumps.

I hang the bandana on the wall above my desk, tell myself it's just decoration, and try not to notice how it makes the whole room feel lighter.

Chapter 14 – Nate

The first thing I see when I open my phone is my own face.

Not a mirror.

On the internet.

Glitter. Hearts. Hashtags.

#HotDogDad

#ReluctantRomeo

#DoubleDogDateYa

I scroll. There's a video of me and Sienna laughing while Diesel rolls between us. Someone's added music—Barry White.

"Oh for God's sake."

Diesel barks once, tail thumping, like he personally edited it.

"Yeah, laugh it up, Spielberg."

A headline flashes on my feed: Wall Street Wolf Tamed by Yogi Queen.

I almost drop my coffee. Ziggy's fingerprints are all over this.

Before I can text him death threats, the phone rings.

"Morning, superstar," Jax says, voice half-asleep, half-amused.

"Don't start."

"I saw the video. You've got chemistry."

"With Diesel?"

"With the yoga lady."

"Sienna," I correct before I can stop myself.

He laughs. "You remember her name. Cute."

"I remember lawsuits too. This has defamation written all over it."

"Relax, man. You looked happy."

"I looked like a man trapped in a Hallmark commercial."

Jax snorts. "Same thing."

He shows up an hour later at The Yard with breakfast sandwiches and zero mercy. Tank lumbers behind him; Diesel greets him like a long-lost brother.

"All right," Jax says, tossing me a leash. "Let's work that viral-video energy into something useful."

We start obedience drills. Diesel nails every command, because of course he does.

Jax folds his arms. "He listens when you mean it."

"I meant it yesterday."

"You meant to survive yesterday," he says. "Different thing."

I glare. "You always this philosophical before breakfast?"

"Always."

Diesel steals half his sandwich mid-sentence. Jax freezes, staring at the empty wrapper.

I lose it—first a laugh, then a real, aching belly-laugh.

"There it is," Jax says, grinning. "Proof of life, part two."

"Don't get used to it."

"Oh I will."

He points at my phone on the bench. "By the way, Ziggy's interview drops at noon."

"What interview?"

"The one where he called you The Reluctant Romeo of Rescue Romance."

I choke on my coffee. "He did not."

"He did. And he announced Round Two next weekend."

"Perfect."

"Hey," Jax says, clapping my shoulder. "Maybe you're good for each other."

"Me and Ziggy?"

He smirks. "You and Sienna."

I open my mouth for a comeback, but Diesel lets out a sharp bark, like he's voting yes.

I point at him. "Don't encourage this."

Tank grumbles. Jax laughs.

When they finally leave, I sit on the training bench scrolling through photos again. Sienna's laugh—caught mid-sunlight, genuine, unguarded—hits harder than it should.

I tell myself I'm going to Round Two to prove a point.

The point's still fuzzy, but it starts with her laugh.

Chapter 15 – Sienna

By nine a.m., the park looks like a dog-themed fairground again.

The pup-cake truck's parked under the big oak, Ziggy's in a sequined blazer that could signal ships, and Lila's already regretting every decision that led her here.

"Welcome to Double Dog Date Ya 2: Electric Bark-aloo!" Ziggy hollers through a megaphone. "Find love, find fur, find yourself!"

Lila mutters, "I find migraines."

I laugh, but my stomach's a knot of nerves. Everything looks perfect—banners, tables, the check-in booth—but my brain keeps circling one question: Will he actually show up?

Then he does.

Nate Callahan in a gray T-shirt that's somehow both casual and criminal, walking like he's braced for combat. Diesel trots beside him, tail high, already scanning for me.

Great. Even the dog's punctual.

"Don't stare," Lila says, elbowing me.

"I'm not."

"You are."

Before I can argue, Diesel spots me and barrels forward.

I'm holding a coffee; of course it happens in slow motion.

Eighty pounds of enthusiasm collides with caffeine.

The cup explodes. My clipboard becomes modern art.

"Oh—" I start, but Nate's already there, hands steadying my elbow. When his fingers brush my wrist I catch, faint and calming, lavender—like a quiet pocket of air that doesn't belong to the chaos.

"Guess he missed you," he says, half-smile curling.

"I noticed."

Diesel drops to the grass, tail thumping, proud of the carnage.

Lila snorts. "That's one way to make an entrance." She drifts off muttering something about towels.

Nate grabs a napkin from the vendor table and hands it to me. "You okay?"

"Fine," I say, blotting my shirt. "It's organic. I'll survive."

He grins. "You sure? That looked like a high-velocity latte."

I can't help it; I laugh. "You're impossible."

"Accurate," he says. "But at least I'm consistent."

Ziggy appears at our side like a caffeinated genie.

"Lennon! Callahan! The crowd's ready for Round Two introductions!"

"Ziggy, I swear—"

"Relax," he whispers, sliding his sunglasses up. "You two are trending again. Play along. The dogs demand it."

Before I can argue, he grabs Nate's shoulder and spins us toward the mic.

"Round Two!" he announces. "The Rematch! The redemption arc none of us saw coming!"

The crowd cheers. Diesel barks on cue. Nate groans.

I stand there, caught between horror and laughter. Ziggy hands me the mic.

"Say something inspiring, Lennon."

"I—uh—hope everyone remembered poop bags?"

The crowd laughs; Ziggy claps like I've given a TED Talk.

Then he whispers, "You're a natural," and bolts off to orchestrate more chaos.

A few minutes later I'm at the registration table, trying to refill my coffee when Nate reappears.

Diesel's leash tangles with the rope line. I bend to untangle it just as he does.

We meet halfway; hands brush. Static. Real this time.

"Sorry," I murmur.

He clears his throat. "You first."

We both step the same direction, then the other.

Ziggy yells from somewhere, "The universe ships it!"

The crowd laughs.

I shake my head, smiling despite myself. "I'm going to kill him."

"Get in line," Nate says.

We finish untangling the leash, but the air between us stays tight and humming.

He starts to say something, then stops.

"What?" I ask.

He shrugs. "Nothing. You just look—different."

"Covered in coffee?"

He smiles. "Happy. Even with the coffee."

It's such a simple thing, but it lodges under my ribs.

He hesitates a beat longer, voice lower. "I wasn't always like this."

"Like what?"

"Detached. Avoidant. Pick an adjective."

He looks out toward the park, where Diesel's circling a vendor table. "There was someone—Gracie. We were engaged. She died in a car crash."

My throat tightens. "Oh. Nate, I'm so sorry."

He gives the smallest shake of his head. "It was a long time ago. But she was… the last time I tried to build something permanent."

There's no drama in his tone, just a quiet honesty that hums like grief learned to live beside him.

"I get that," I say softly.

He meets my eyes. "Do you?"

"Loss leaves cracks," I answer. "But sometimes that's where the light finds you."

For a second neither of us moves. Then Diesel barks at a passing pug and the spell breaks.

He smiles faintly. "Thanks, Lennon."

"Don't mention it," I say, even though I'll probably think about it all night.

The event rolls on in a blur of barking and laughter. Ziggy poses for selfies, Lila handles donations, and I float from table to table pretending not to look for him even when I know exactly where he is.

Every time Diesel finds me, Nate's there a second later.

It's a dance neither of us planned but both keep doing.

When the final whistle blows, Diesel flops beside my feet, tongue lolling, tail wagging. Nate stops beside us, hands in his pockets.

"Looks like he picked a favorite."

"Maybe he just likes the pup-cakes."

"Yeah," he says. "Me too."

And there it is—that tiny spark that feels like trouble and hope tangled together, just like our leashes.

Chapter 16 – Nate

I've spent most of my adult life avoiding two things:

commitment and glitter.

And thanks to Double Dog Date Ya, I've been assaulted by both.

The event wrapped up hours ago, but I'm still finding glitter on my shirt, in my car, probably in my soul.

Diesel's asleep in the passenger seat, tongue lolling, reeking faintly of frosting.

I swear he's smiling again.

"You realize you're the problem, right?" I tell him.

He doesn't move. Typical.

I pull into the garage, kill the engine, and just sit there.

I should be thinking about work—numbers, deals, anything logical—but instead my brain keeps replaying one image on a loop:

Sienna's laugh when Diesel toppled the treat table.

Soft at first, then full, honest.

She looked free.

I don't think I've ever looked like that in my life.

"Don't start," I mutter, hauling myself out of the car. "She's yoga. You're chaos. End of story."

Diesel follows me upstairs, immediately noses my jacket pocket, and drags out a half-crushed pup-cake.

"Disgusting," I say, even as I hand it to him.

My phone buzzes.

A text from Ziggy. Of course.

ZIGGY: Congrats, Loverboy! The internet ships you!

ME: Delete it before I sue you.

ZIGGY: You can't sue destiny.

ME: Watch me.

ZIGGY: Also, the rescue doubled donations. You're welcome.

I toss the phone on the couch and drop beside Diesel, who lets out a contented sigh.

He's glowing—tail twitching, belly up, blissed out.

He's in love.

Fantastic.

My dog's having a better emotional life than I am.

The next morning, I'm at The Yard again.

Jax is already there, Tank lumbering at his side.

"You're early," he says, surprised.

"Couldn't sleep."

"Uh-huh." He tosses a ball. "Because of a dog or a woman?"

"Neither. Indigestion."

"Sure."

He gives me that knowing grin that makes me want to find another trainer.

Diesel's bounding across the dirt, energy to spare.

I watch him and remember Sienna crouched beside him, rubbing his ear, murmuring something that made him melt.

It's irritating—the way her voice keeps replaying in my head like a song I didn't mean to like.

Jax whistles. "He's different."

"What do you mean?"

"Looser. Happier. More confident." He glances at me. "Dogs mirror their owners, you know."

"Great," I deadpan. "Now we're both in denial."

He laughs. "You could just admit you like her."

"Not my type."

"Remind me—your type again?"

"Unavailable."

He tosses the ball harder. "Then you're doomed, man."

By afternoon, I'm at my desk pretending to work.

The monitor glows with spreadsheets; my brain hums with chaos.

I can't concentrate.

Every time I blink, I see her—

the way she grinned at Diesel,

the way she looked at me like she was waiting for something I didn't know how to give.

The phone buzzes again—another text from Ziggy.

ZIGGY: You're trending again. Also, there's talk of Round Three. Bigger crowds, more sponsors, maybe national coverage.

I type: No chance.

Then delete it.

Then type: We'll see.

Diesel lifts his head, ears perked like he knows exactly what I wrote.

"Don't look at me like that," I say. "It's for charity."

He yawns, unimpressed.

That night, as I'm locking up, I glance at the couch.

Diesel's asleep with his head on that same red bandana Sienna always carries in her rescue photos.

I have no idea how he got it.

Probably Ziggy. Or fate. Or both.

I stand there longer than I should, looking at it.

At him.

At the glitter still clinging to my sleeve.

I tell myself I'll call Ziggy tomorrow to shut it down.

But I already know I won't.

Chapter 17 – Sienna

I've spent three days reminding myself that attraction is not a symptom of progress.

It's Tuesday, the rescue's quiet, and I'm determined to keep it that way.

No charity carnivals, no glitter, no emotionally confusing men.

Just yoga mats, dogs, and peace.

Ziggy bursts through the front door wearing a T-shirt that says Namast'ay in Love.

So much for peace.

"Morning, Lennon!" he sings. "How's our local celebrity?"

"Busy," I answer, moving a box of leashes onto the shelf. "And not a celebrity."

He holds up his phone. "Tell that to your fan mail. Someone crocheted a portrait of you and Nate hugging Diesel. It's disturbingly detailed."

"Delete it."

"Too late. I printed it for the rescue wall."

"Ziggy."

"Relax," he says, flopping onto a yoga bolster. "You look great in yarn."

I exhale through my nose—the only safe response when logic fails. "Please tell me you're here for something useful."

"Oh, I am." His grin widens. "We're adding a Dog & Human Yoga class next week—fundraiser part three. I already put you down to teach."

"Absolutely not."

"Too late. Posters are at the printer."

I pinch the bridge of my nose. "Do you ever ask before manifesting?"

"Not when the universe says yes first."

Lila pokes her head from the office. "Also, Callahan signed up."

"What?" It comes out sharper than I mean. "When?"

"About ten minutes ago," she says. "Ziggy sent him the link."

Ziggy throws up jazz hands. "Fate! You two are yin and yang—except you're the peaceful one and he's the part that needs stretching."

"Ziggy—"

He's already halfway out the door, humming something that sounds suspiciously like a wedding march.

Later, after the last adoption appointment, I'm setting up mats for the evening class.

The rescue's quiet except for the low hum of the heater and the occasional tail thump against a kennel.

The stillness feels good—safe.

Then my phone buzzes.

NATE CALLAHAN: Is there a dress code for dog yoga? Asking for Diesel.

ME: If he's not wearing pants, he's fine.

NATE: Good. Because I don't own yoga pants.

ME: Then maybe skip the downward dog.

The typing bubbles appear, disappear, reappear.

NATE: You sure you want me in your class?

My thumbs hover. I should say no. I should protect my peace.

ME: It's for charity.

NATE: That's what you always say right before chaos.

ME: Then at least it's familiar.

I set the phone down and realize I'm smiling.

When I lock up that night, I glance at the red bandana still hanging above my desk.

The dogs are asleep, the lights are low, and the air smells faintly of lavender and wet fur.

"Just yoga," I tell myself.

But it doesn't sound convincing, even to me.

Chapter 18 – Nate

If there's a hell designed specifically for men like me, it probably involves yoga mats.

Class hasn't even started and I already feel ridiculous—barefoot, surrounded by people who look like they stepped out of a wellness catalog. Diesel sits proudly beside me, tail sweeping, as if he's ready for enlightenment.

"Don't look at me like that," I whisper. "You're the one who dragged me here."

Across the room, Sienna kneels on a mat, arranging candles along the front edge. Her hair's in a loose braid, a few strands against her cheek, and I swear the room smells like her—lavender and something faintly sweet.

She looks up, catches me watching. Raises one eyebrow.

I look away like I wasn't staring. Smooth, Callahan.

"Okay, everyone," she says, voice calm, warm. "Welcome to Dog & Human Yoga. Find your mat, find your breath, and remember—if your dog decides to nap or wander, that's part of the practice."

Ziggy's in the back filming with his phone, whisper-narrating like we're on a nature show. "Observe the reluctant male in his natural habitat—attempting tranquility."

I shoot him a glare. He blows me a kiss.

Sienna starts the warm-up. "Let's begin in mountain pose. Feet grounded, shoulders relaxed."

I try. Diesel decides my left foot is the ideal spot to sit on.

"Breathe in," she says.

I inhale.

"Breathe out."

Diesel burps.

A few people giggle. Sienna's mouth twitches, fighting a smile.

"Perfect," she says. "That's grounding energy."

She moves to the next pose—downward dog, of course. Because the universe has a sense of humor.

I attempt it. My hamstrings file a formal complaint.

Diesel mirrors me perfectly, tail wagging under my face like a metronome of mockery.

Sienna walks by, adjusting posture. When she reaches me, she rests a hand lightly on my back.

"Breathe here," she murmurs.

Her voice is soft enough that it hits somewhere deeper than my lungs.

For a second, I forget what air is.

Then Diesel chooses that exact moment to crawl under me and lick my face.

The class erupts. I collapse onto the mat, sputtering. "You planned that," I tell him.

Sienna's laughing too—really laughing, hand over her mouth. The sound's worth every ounce of humiliation.

"Diesel's demonstrating vulnerability," she says once she can breathe again.

"Yeah? He can demonstrate obedience next."

"Unlikely," she says, smiling down at me.

She offers a hand to help me up. I take it, and for a beat longer than necessary, neither of us lets go.

Halfway through class, the dogs are sprawled across mats like tiny gurus. Diesel's asleep with his head on Sienna's foot.

I whisper, "He's a traitor."

She whispers back, "He's an empath."

When we move into the final stretch—lying on our backs, eyes closed—her voice softens even more. "Let your breath settle. Feel the connection between you and your dog— trust without words."

I peek. Her eyes are closed, face relaxed, peaceful.

Something inside me goes completely still.

I close my eyes too, and for once, the silence doesn't feel empty.

After class, people linger, chatting, leashes tangling. Ziggy buzzes around collecting donations and trying to sell sage bundles.

Sienna's rolling up mats when I walk over.

"You survived," she says.

"Barely. I think my spine filed for divorce."

She laughs. "You did great. Diesel's a natural."

"Yeah, he's been showing off ever since he met you."

"Smart dog."

She glances up, eyes meeting mine. Not teasing—warmer, curious.

"Thanks for coming," she says.

I shrug. "Charity, right?"

"Sure," she says, smiling like she doesn't believe me.

Diesel nudges her hand for a pat, and she bends, rubbing his ears. When she looks up again, she's close enough that I can smell lavender on her skin.

"See you next time?" she asks.

"Probably," I hear myself say.

Ziggy materializes with a donation jar. "You two are poetry in motion. I'm thinking Doggy Date: The Movie!"

"Don't push it," I say, but Sienna's laughing again.

Diesel barks, tail wagging, sealing the deal.

That night, after I drop Diesel at home, I catch myself checking the rescue's event calendar.

Just once.

Or maybe twice.

Charity, I tell myself.

Definitely charity.

Chapter 19 – Sienna

I've taught hundreds of classes. CEOs through breathing, brides through pre-wedding jitters. Even a poodle in a tutu once.

But no one—no one—has ever thrown off my balance like Nate Callahan.

It's been two hours since class ended, and I'm still replaying it like a movie I didn't mean to like.

The way he tried to look unimpressed and failed.

The way he laughed when Diesel knocked him flat.

The way his hand felt—steady, calloused, surprisingly gentle—when he helped me up.

"Don't do this," I tell myself, pacing the studio while wiping down mats. "He's not your type. He's your fundraiser."

From the doorway, Ziggy answers like a ghost who's always eavesdropping. "Labels are limitations, Lennon."

I drop the spray bottle. "Do you rehearse these entrances?"

"Spontaneity is my gift." He glides in, sniffing the air. "Smells like love and disinfectant. My two favorite auras."

"Please stop sniffing."

"Can't. It's destiny." He flops onto a mat. "So, how was class?"

"Fine."

"Define fine."

"No fatalities."

He props his chin on his hands. "Did he breathe?"

"Yes."

"Did you?"

"Ziggy."

He grins. "Ah, so there was breathlessness. Excellent."

I glare. "You are not allowed near my emotional state without a permit."

"Too late, I forged one." He sits up. "He likes you, Lennon. I can feel it."

"Diesel likes everyone."

"Not Diesel, dummy. Nate."

I whip a towel at him. "Out."

He dodges easily. "Lila's going to be thrilled. Our reluctant lovers, finding enlightenment through core strength."

"I'm serious."

"So am I. You've been smiling since he left."

I freeze mid-wipe. "No, I haven't."

He points at my reflection in the mirror. He's right. There's a small, traitorous curve at the corner of my mouth.

"Ugh," I say, covering it with my hand. "It's residual serotonin from exercise."

"Sure, Lennon. Keep telling yourself that."

Later that night, I sit at my kitchen table with a mug of tea and my notebook open.

The next fundraiser idea should be spilling out—logistics, dates, sponsors.

Instead, my pen hovers uselessly while my brain replays one memory: Nate, lying on his mat, Diesel licking his face while the room laughed.

The sound of his laugh—low, rough, surprised—hit me somewhere I didn't expect.

Like a memory of something I haven't had in years.

Safety.

Warmth.

Maybe even joy.

I shut the notebook. "Nope."

My phone buzzes. A text.

NATE: Diesel says thanks for class. He achieved enlightenment halfway through savasana.

I bite back a smile.

ME: Tell him to teach you next time.

NATE: I think he's trying.

ME: Good luck. He's stubborn.

NATE: Takes one to know one.

I stare at the screen longer than I should. Then I type:

ME: You're impossible.

He replies instantly.

NATE: And yet here we are.

Ziggy's words echo: You've been smiling since he left.

Fine.

Maybe I am.

Just a little.

Chapter 20 – Nate

Diesel has been staring at my phone for ten straight minutes.

I swear he knows what I'm doing—or not doing.

"Stop judging me," I say.

He yawns, flops over, and deliberately knocks the phone off the coffee table with one paw.

"Great. Now you're my conscience."

I pick it up again. The last text from Sienna still glows on the screen: You're impossible.

I should leave it there. Neat ending. Full stop.

Instead I type: You started it.

Delete.

Type again: Diesel misses yoga.

Delete.

Finally I toss the phone aside like it's dangerous, which, technically, it is.

At The Yard, Jax is hosing down the concrete when I walk in. Tank and Diesel race circles in the mud, both looking way too happy for Monday.

"You're early," he says.

"I couldn't sleep."

"Let me guess—spreadsheets?"

"Sure. Spreadsheets. That's what keeps me up at night."

He chuckles. "You got it bad."

"I don't have anything."

"Except insomnia, denial, and a dog who's wagging like he just got a Valentine."

I glare. "You talking to Ziggy again?"

"He doesn't have to tell me. It's written all over your face."

"What's written on my face is mind your own business."

Jax hands me a broom. "Fine. Sweep your denial into a neat little pile."

We work in silence—me sweeping, him pretending not to watch. Finally he says,

"You know what your problem is, Callahan? You keep thinking love's an equation you can solve."

"And you think it's what, divine chaos?"

"Exactly. And Diesel's already solved it for you."

Diesel trots by, carrying Sienna's red bandana in his mouth. I have no idea where he found it again.

"See?" Jax says. "Even the dog's manifesting."

"Remind me to fire Ziggy for teaching you that word."

Later that afternoon, I'm back in my office pretending to work. My inbox is full of actual business, but every few minutes my cursor drifts toward my phone.

When it finally buzzes, I nearly drop it.

SIENNA: Quick question—does Diesel eat peanut butter?

Relief, adrenaline—something.

ME: He'd sell me for a jar of it.

SIENNA: Good. I'm making treats for the rescue event.

ME: You bribing him or me?

SIENNA: Whichever works faster.

ME: Then you're in trouble.

…typing…

SIENNA: Maybe I like trouble.

I stare at that one until my screen goes dark.

That night, Diesel climbs onto the couch, rests his head on my leg, and sighs like he's finally got the world figured out.

I run a hand over his fur, the motion automatic.

"Don't get attached," I tell him. "This isn't a thing."

He thumps his tail once, slow and knowing.

"Fine," I mutter. "Maybe it's a little bit of a thing."

The TV's still on mute, cycling through the local news. I glance up just as a human-interest segment starts— coverage of the Double Dog Date Ya fundraiser. Sienna's in the background, talking to a reporter beside a group of rescue volunteers.

And then I see him.

A man standing a few feet behind her, half-turned toward
the camera. The name tag on his shirt reads Monroe.

My pulse stutters. It's an old, sharp recognition—the kind
that lives in your gut, not your memory.

I know that face. From a case file. From headlines I swore
I'd stopped reading.

Before the sound can catch up, I mute the TV completely.
Diesel lifts his head, confused.

"It's nothing," I lie, the words tasting wrong.

I sit there until the segment ends, watching the reflection of
the dark screen.

The city hums through the windows, low and steady.

For the first time since Gracie's crash, the quiet doesn't feel
empty—

it feels dangerous.

Chapter 21 – Sienna

The kitchen smells like peanut butter, honey, and disaster.

There's flour on the counter, on my jeans, and somehow in my hair.

Diesel's bandana—yes, that bandana—is tied around my ponytail to keep it out of the batter. The irony is not lost on me.

"Don't look at me like that," I tell the foster pup sitting at my feet.

She blinks slowly, unimpressed, as I drop another tray of half-baked dog treats onto the cooling rack.

Lila wanders in, mug in hand, eyes wide.

"Are we making cookies or staging a food fight?"

"Fundraiser prep," I say. "And maybe emotional regulation."

She grins. "So… baking therapy."

"Exactly."

She picks up a treat, sniffs it. "These actually smell amazing."

"Peanut butter, oat flour, honey, and guilt."

"Guilt?"

"I might have flirted with Nate Callahan over text."

Lila nearly chokes on her coffee. "You what?"

"It was an accident."

"You don't accidentally flirt, Lennon. You've been celibate since the Obama administration."

I throw a towel at her. "Thank you for that history lesson."

She laughs, perching on the counter. "So what'd he say?"

"Nothing, really." I stir the next bowl harder than necessary. "He joked, I joked. There might've been a 'maybe I like trouble' comment."

"Oh my God, he so likes you."

"It's just banter."

"Uh-huh."

She sips her coffee, smug. "Banter is flirting for people in denial."

Before I can reply, my phone buzzes.

Diesel's photo lights up the screen—Ziggy must have saved Nate's number that way.

Lila waves me off. "Answer it."

I do, mostly to shut her up. "Hey."

His voice is warm, rough with a smile. "Hey yourself. Diesel wanted to know if you needed a taste tester."

"Does Diesel talk often, or just when he's angling for treats?"

"Only when the bribes are this good."

I laugh, even though I try not to. "He'll get a whole batch."

"And me?"

I pause, heartbeat stuttering. "You can have one. If you behave."

"Define behave."

"I'll let you know when you're doing it."

He laughs—low, genuine. It hits somewhere deep and unfamiliar.

"Thanks for the heads-up," he says. "I'll try to earn my cookie."

"Good luck."

He hesitates. "You sound happy."

I glance around at the mess—flour, barking, the smell of warm peanut butter—and smile. "Maybe I am."

"Good," he says quietly. "You should be."

For a moment neither of us speaks. Then he clears his throat. "Okay, before Ziggy calls and starts planning our wedding, I should go."

I laugh. "Wise choice."

"See you Saturday?"

"See you Saturday."

When the call ends, the kitchen feels brighter somehow.

Lila's grinning like a cat who knows too much. "So, cookies and chemistry. My favorite combo."

"Don't," I warn.

She holds up her mug. "Too late. I ship it."

That night, I sit on the couch with a sleeping pup in my lap, scrolling through photos from the last event. There's one of Nate holding Diesel's leash, squinting against the sun, smiling at something off-camera.

Me, probably.

I should delete it.

Instead, I favorite it.

Chapter 22 – Nate

For the first time in years, the apartment smells like something other than takeout and regret.

Peanut butter.

Diesel's on the couch, licking his paws and sighing like a man who just closed a good deal.

A paper bag from the rescue sits on the coffee table— Sienna's dog treats. She dropped them off earlier, apparently while I was still at work.

Or at least that's what Ziggy texted: "Sienna left love in snack form. Don't screw it up."

The note on top of the bag reads, For Diesel. Try not to steal them all, signed with a doodle of a paw print.

I pick up one of the treats. Diesel stares like it's made of gold.

"You get the first one," I tell him. "You earned it."

He crunches it, tail thumping, eyes half-closed in bliss.

I take another out, just looking at it—peanut butter, oats, honey. Simple. Homemade.

It's the first time in forever someone's made something with my name attached to it, even by accident.

"Don't look at me like that," I mutter. "I'm not sentimental."

Diesel doesn't blink. He knows better.

My phone buzzes. A message from Ziggy.

ZIGGY: Did you eat the love cookies?

ME: They're for Diesel.

ZIGGY: Love is a group activity, Nate.

ME: Stop texting me.

ZIGGY: Too late. Also, she looked happy today.

I set the phone face-down.

That last sentence lands somewhere I don't expect—quiet, but heavy.

I grab my jacket and Diesel's leash. "Come on, partner. Let's get some air."

We walk through the park where the first event was held. The lights from the pup-cake truck are long gone, but the grass still holds the faint imprint of all those blankets and laughter.

Diesel trots ahead, nose to the ground. He stops by the oak where we sat—same spot, same patch of worn grass.

He sits. Looks up at me.

"What?" I ask.

He tilts his head, then barks once—sharp, decisive.

"You expect me to text her, don't you?"

Another bark.

"You're relentless."

He pants, victorious.

I pull out my phone before I can think better of it.

ME: The treats were a hit. Diesel wants your recipe. I want to hire your marketing team.

SIENNA: Tell Diesel I accept payment in belly rubs.

ME: You or him?

SIENNA: Both, probably.

I grin despite myself.

ME: Deal.

Back at the apartment, Diesel curls up beside me on the couch. The city hums outside—soft and distant.

I glance at the bag of cookies again. It shouldn't mean anything, but somehow it does.

For the first time in a long time, the quiet doesn't feel like loneliness.

It feels like waiting—for something good.

Chapter 23 – Sienna

I've been staring at a blank page for twenty minutes.

Technically, it's a planning worksheet for the next fundraiser. Realistically, it's a mirror reflecting one undeniable truth: my brain has been hijacked by a man and his dog.

"Focus," I mutter, scribbling new sponsors? across the top.

Ziggy appears upside-down in the reflection of my laptop screen. "Talking to yourself now? Excellent. That's the first step toward enlightenment—or insanity. They're cousins."

I turn. "Do you materialize out of sage smoke?"

He grins. "Always." He's holding two iced coffees and an obnoxiously pink pastry box. "Peace offerings from the food-truck couple. They're still glowing from the event."

I take the coffee gratefully. "Tell them thank you."

"They said to tell you you're their 'patron saint of second chances.' Also, they made a dog-friendly doughnut called the Karma Kruller."

"Of course they did."

He flops into a chair. "So. What's next? Round Three? Love Unleashed: The Sequel?"

"Not yet." I try to sound firm. "We need to regroup. Strategize."

He tilts his head. "You mean overthink."

"I mean plan."

"Tomato, tomahto."

Before I can argue, Lila breezes in with a stack of mail. "Morning, lovebirds."

"Good morning," Ziggy and I say in unison, then glare at each other.

She laughs. "Relax. I was talking about the dogs on the postcard. But interesting reaction."

"I am not a lovebird," I protest.

Ziggy sips his coffee. "Denial—my second-favorite flavor."

Lila drops the mail on my desk. "Oh, look. A handwritten note from a donor."

I open the envelope. Inside is a simple card covered in neat handwriting:

Thank you for bringing joy back to the park. Watching everyone laugh—and watching you laugh—reminded me what hope looks like.

— N.C.

My heart does that embarrassing lurch it shouldn't still be capable of.

Ziggy leans in, reading over my shoulder. "Ohhh, the brooding billionaire writes letters now."

I smack his arm with the envelope. "Personal space!"

"He's evolving," Ziggy says solemnly. "Next he'll discover emojis."

Lila's smiling knowingly. "He's a good one, Sienna."

I fold the note carefully, tucking it into my planner. "He's complicated."

"So are you," she says gently. "Maybe that's the point."

That evening, the rescue's quiet. The dogs are fed, the lights are low, and I'm sorting adoption files when my phone buzzes.

NATE: Diesel says thanks for the treats. He also says he misses yoga.

I smile.

ME: Tell Diesel I'll schedule him a private session.

NATE: And the human?

ME: Depends. Can he follow instructions yet?

NATE: Working on it.

I stare at his last message until the words blur a little.

Working on it.

Me too.

Chapter 24 – Nate

The city outside my window is a blur of light and rain.

Normally I'd be finishing reports—or pretending to—but tonight the laptop's open only because I like the glow.

Diesel's on the couch, head on his paws, watching me like a slow-motion train wreck.

The bag of Sienna's peanut-butter cookies sits on the coffee table between us.

"Don't even think about it," I say.

He blinks once, then inches a paw toward the bag.

I sigh. "Fine. One more. We both need serotonin."

He crunches happily, crumbs everywhere.

When he's done, he noses the folded note that came with the bag. I grab it before he can slobber on it.

It's her handwriting—neat, confident, looping a little at the edges.

Thanks for helping us keep the tails wagging.

— Sienna

I've read it three times. Four, maybe. I keep telling myself it's just manners, but my brain doesn't buy it.

Diesel climbs onto the couch beside me, tail thumping once.

"Yeah, I know," I say. "You miss her."

He licks my cheek—confirmation.

I lean back, stare at the ceiling. The apartment's still except for the rain tapping the windows. Usually the quiet feels like punishment; tonight it's a reprieve.

My phone buzzes. Another text from her.

SIENNA: The shelter's lights are flickering again. Ziggy says it's ghosts. I say it's bad wiring. Thoughts?

ME: Probably both. You should call an electrician. Or a priest.

SIENNA: You volunteering?

ME: Depends. Do I get hazard pay?

SIENNA: You get coffee and company.

I stare at the message. The cursor blinks like a heartbeat.

ME: Tomorrow morning work for you?

She replies almost instantly.

SIENNA: See you then.

Diesel wags his tail so hard the couch shakes.

I scratch behind his ear. "Don't get ahead of yourself. It's just coffee."

He gives me the canine equivalent of a smirk.

"Fine," I admit, tossing him another cookie. "Maybe it's not just coffee."

Later, when the lights are off and the city hum fades, I lie awake with that ridiculous smile still hanging around.

The ache that used to live in my chest—Gracie, my dad, all of it—feels quieter now, like someone finally turned the volume down.

Maybe that's what Sienna does. She doesn't fix things; she just makes the noise stop.

For the first time in longer than I can remember, I'm not dreading tomorrow.

I'm waiting for it.

Chapter 25 – Sienna

By the time I unlock the studio door the next morning, Ziggy's already there—balancing on a ladder, waving a bundle of smoldering sage like a sword.

"Begone, energy vampires!" he declares to the light fixtures.

"Good morning," I say dryly, setting my bag on the counter. "And by vampires, you mean…?"

"Faulty wiring," he says, hopping down. "But a little spiritual maintenance never hurts. Oh—Callahan called. Said he's on his way."

My heart does a tiny, traitorous flip.

"Here? Why?"

"To check the wiring." He air-quotes. "Pretty sure that's electrician code for romantic subtext."

"Ziggy."

He grins, eyes twinkling. "Just saying—wear something that says I'm open to new circuits."

I throw him a towel. "You're incorrigible."

"That's Latin for you love me," he says, vanishing into the office.

Ten minutes later, Nate walks in carrying two coffees and a toolbox that looks like it hasn't been opened since the Bush administration.

Diesel trots beside him, happy as ever.

"Morning," he says, handing me one of the cups. "For the wiring consultant."

"Appreciated. I charge extra for emergencies."

He smirks. "I brought donuts as backup."

"You're learning," I say, taking a sip. It's exactly how I like it—strong, two sugars.

Coincidence? Probably. Maybe.

Diesel sniffs the corners of the room like he's inspecting for spirits.

When he looks up at me and wags, the overhead light flickers once.

Ziggy's head pops out of the office. "See? Validation!"

"Pretty sure that's the ballast," Nate says.

"Ballast, ghost—tomato, tomahto," Ziggy answers, disappearing again.

I shake my head. "Welcome to my mornings."

Nate grins. "It's… not boring."

"No," I say. "Boring would be a nice change."

He crouches by the fuse box, flipping switches with practiced confidence.

"How do you even know how to do that?"

"My dad was a cop," he says. "He didn't fix feelings, but he fixed everything else."

The air goes still for a beat. He glances up, something quiet and honest in his eyes.

I swallow. "Well, your wiring diagnosis is spot-on. It's been like this for weeks."

He shrugs. "Loose connection. Nothing major."

"Good. We've had enough chaos lately."

"Chaos builds character," he says, smiling a little.

"You would know."

He laughs under his breath. "You wound me."

"Only slightly," I tease, handing him a donut from the bag.

He takes it. Our fingers brush—small, but real.

Diesel flops onto a mat near Ziggy's incense, groaning like he's found nirvana.

Ziggy reappears with his phone. "I need a picture of this energy."

"Don't even—" I start.

"Too late!" Click. "Perfect. Candid. Caffeine. Chemistry."

"Delete it," I warn.

"Never," he says, backing toward the door. "I'm sending it to Lila. She'll cry."

"Ziggy!"

He disappears again, humming something suspiciously like a wedding march.

When the chaos settles, it's just the three of us—me, Nate, and Diesel, sprawled on the mat, half-asleep.

The lights are steady now, warm against the studio walls.

"Looks like you fixed it," I say softly.

He nods. "Guess I'm good for something after all."

I smile. "I could've told you that."

He glances over, eyes meeting mine. "Yeah?"

"Yeah."

For a moment, no one moves. The air hums—electricity finally finding its path.

Then Diesel lets out a loud snore, breaking the spell.

We both laugh—too hard—tension dissolving into something easy.

When he leaves, the studio feels too quiet.

There's still a faint smell of sage and coffee in the air, and one donut sits untouched on the counter.

I stare at it for a long time, then smile.

"Fine," I whisper to no one. "Maybe chaos does build character."

Chapter 26 – Nate

The day after the "wiring job," I can't concentrate on anything.

My inbox looks like a math problem I refuse to solve.

Every subject line blurs into the same sentence: You're distracted.

They're not wrong.

Diesel's asleep at my feet, one paw twitching like he's chasing something in his dreams—probably Sienna's dog biscuits.

Every time I glance at the coffee mug on my desk, I remember the one she handed me yesterday. Same brand, same smell, completely different effect.

By lunch, I give up and drive to The Yard.

Jax is repairing a fence, Tank dozing in the shade. He looks up when I slam the truck door.

"Afternoon, Romeo."

"Don't start."

He smirks. "Ziggy posted your little repair session. #LoveAtFirstCircuit is trending."

"Kill me."

"Too late. The internet's already done it for you."

I grab a hammer just to have something to hold. "Remind me why I put up with him again?"

"Because he's the only person crazy enough to get you out of your head."

He leans against the post, eyes sharp but kind. "You still thinking about her?"

"No," I lie automatically.

"Then why are you here instead of Wall Street?"

I shrug. "Because the market's fine and my dog likes the smell of manure."

Jax laughs. "Sure. Tell yourself that."

He whistles for Diesel, who trots over with a stick bigger than his head.

"See?" Jax says. "He's bringing you signs now. Literally."

I look down. The stick's shaped almost perfectly like a crooked heart.

I drop it. "Coincidence."

Jax just smiles. "You ever think maybe you're allowed to be happy?"

"Happy's overrated."

"Not when you've been miserable this long."

He walks off before I can come up with a comeback.

That night, Diesel and I stop by the park. The lights are low, the city hum soft around us.

I toss a ball once, twice. He doesn't chase it. He just sits, watching the path that leads toward the rescue.

"Yeah," I say quietly. "I miss her too."

My phone buzzes. A text from Ziggy.

ZIGGY: Good news! Channel 7's covering the next fundraiser. They want an interview with our power couple—tomorrow. Prime time.

ME: No.

ZIGGY: Yes.

ME: Absolutely not.

ZIGGY: Diesel already said yes.

I groan. "You'd betray me that easily?" I ask Diesel.

He barks once, tail wagging.

"Fine," I mutter. "One interview. Then I'm done."

Except we both know I'm not.

Later, back at the apartment, I stare out at the skyline. The city glitters—too bright, too busy—but somehow it doesn't feel like noise tonight.

It feels like anticipation.

Maybe Jax is right. Maybe I'm allowed to be happy.

Maybe she's the reason I finally want to be.

Chapter 27 – Sienna

Ziggy bursts through the rescue doors like a game-show host announcing the grand prize.

"Lennon! Pack your best aura—we're going on TV!"

I blink. "It's nine a.m., and I haven't even had coffee."

He shoves a tablet in my face. On the screen: a local-news email thread with too many exclamation points.

Subject: LIVE SEGMENT – 'Double Dog Date Ya' Success Story

"They want us! A real-time love-and-rescue story. You, Nate, Diesel. Tomorrow. Prime time!"

Lila looks up from the counter, already mouthing oh no.

"I can't do live television," I say. "My voice gets weird. I blink too much."

"Blinking is authentic!" Ziggy declares. "Viewers crave authenticity."

"Authenticity also sweats," Lila adds.

Ziggy ignores her. "This is fate, Lennon. The universe is handing you a microphone—and possibly a lighting crew."

I take the tablet, scrolling through the details.

One short interview. Live from the park. Focus on rescue funding and the human-dog connection.

The human-dog connection.

Translation: me and Nate on camera, pretending we're not confused by whatever this is.

Lila snorts. "Well, at least you already have chemistry."

"Chemistry isn't the problem," I say. "Combustion is."

By the time the camera crew arrives for a quick test run that afternoon, Ziggy has transformed the park into a rom-com set: fairy lights in the trees, donation jars with glitter hearts, a handmade banner reading LOVE UNLEASHED – LIVE!

"Too much?" he asks.

"Yes," I say. "It's perfect."

Lila chuckles. "Look at you, blushing."

"Heat stroke," I insist.

An hour later, Nate shows up.

Jeans. Gray shirt. A smile he's pretending not to have.

Diesel trots proudly beside him wearing a new collar that gleams in the sun.

"Wow," he says, scanning the lights. "Subtle."

"Ziggy's creative vision," I tell him.

"It's like Cupid exploded."

"Accurate."

He grins. "You ready for your close-up?"

"No," I say honestly.

"Good. Me neither."

For a second we just stand there, side by side, watching Ziggy direct the camera crew like he's Spielberg. It's easy. Comfortable. Dangerous.

Diesel flops between us, sighing like an old married man.

When the crew leaves, Ziggy's still buzzing. "This is it, Lennon! Tomorrow we go viral again. Wear something that says approachable goddess."

Lila leans in. "He's right, you know. This could be huge for the rescue."

I nod, staring at the sunset bleeding across the park.

Huge for the rescue. Terrifying for my sanity.

Because every time Nate looks at me like that—half teasing, half honest—I forget which one of us was supposed to be healing the other.

That night, back home, I open my closet to find something "approachable-goddess-adjacent."

Everything looks wrong. Too soft. Too serious. Too not him.

Then I spot the faded blue shirt from the first event—the one that still smells faintly of lavender and sunlight.

I pull it off the hanger and smile.

"Tomorrow," I whisper, "we'll see if lightning strikes twice."

Chapter 28 – Nate

I should've known the morning was cursed when Diesel stole my tie.

He's parading around the living room with it in his mouth like a victory banner while I'm trying to knot a replacement.

"Give it back."

He wags once. Nope.

"Fine," I mutter, grabbing another. "The blue one makes me look approachable anyway."

The interview's at the park where this whole circus started. Ziggy texted six reminders, three hearts, and a glitter GIF.

By the time I arrive, he's directing the crew like a general at war. "More light! More love! Somebody lint-roll Diesel!"

Sienna's already there—pale-blue shirt again, hair loose, smile tight. She looks calm to everyone else, but I can tell: her fingers keep worrying the corner of a note card.

"You look terrified," I say, handing her coffee.

"I am. You?"

"Terrified's my baseline."

That earns the smallest laugh. Progress.

The producer waves us toward the blanket they've staged under an oak tree. Diesel plops between us, panting happily.

"Just be natural," the reporter says. "Talk about the fundraiser—how you met, why people should donate."

Natural. Right.

The red light blinks on. Microphones hum.

"So, Sienna," the reporter begins, "how did this event start?"

She clears her throat. "It began as a small rescue fundraiser, but it became something bigger—about connection, community, and… dogs teaching humans how to love again."

I glance at her. She's glowing, nervous but genuine—the kind of honest that doesn't need polish.

The reporter turns to me. "And you, Mr. Callahan? What made you get involved?"

Ziggy mouths smile behind the camera.

"I was blackmailed," I say.

Laughter ripples through the crew. Sienna gives me side-eye. "He's joking."

"Half joking," I admit. "But once I showed up, I figured if the dogs were finding second chances, maybe the humans could too."

The reporter beams. "That's beautiful."

"It's accidental," I say, and Sienna elbows me gently.

The reporter gestures toward Diesel. "He seems to be the real star."

"Always," I say. "He saved my life once or twice."

Sienna looks at me, surprised. I hadn't planned to say it, but the words are already out. "My dad's dog. He's smarter than both of us combined."

Her expression softens—quiet understanding passes between us before either of us looks away.

Then Diesel stands, shakes, and flings a perfect arc of drool straight onto the reporter's sleeve.

Everyone freezes.

I choke on a laugh. Sienna loses it first—snorting, doubling over, laughing until the camera operator starts laughing too.

The reporter blinks, then grins. "Well, there's your headline—True Love Is Messy."

Ziggy cheers, "Yes! Keep that energy!"

When it's finally over, the crew applauds. The reporter thanks us for being "so refreshingly real." Diesel basks in the praise like he planned it.

Sienna's still wiping tears of laughter when she looks at me. "You were great."

"Please. I'm going into hiding."

"Too late," she says. "You're officially a heartthrob philanthropist."

"Tragic."

Her smile softens. "You meant what you said, didn't you? About second chances."

I meet her eyes. "Yeah. I think I did."

The space between us hums again—louder now, impossible to ignore.

Then Diesel wedges himself between us, tail wagging, demanding attention.

We both laugh, and somehow that feels like the most honest ending we could give a live broadcast.

That night, the clip hits the internet.

#TrueLoveIsMessy trends within an hour.

I watch it once, twice. Not the drool part—the part right before, where Sienna's hand brushed mine and the whole world looked lighter.

Diesel sighs beside me, head on my knee.

"Yeah," I whisper. "We're in trouble."

The newscast rolls into the next story. My hand freezes on the remote.

Local community hero Monroe Adler partners with city fund to expand rehabilitation programs.

A smiling photo flashes onscreen—Sienna, Ziggy, Lila, and Monroe standing behind the same park banner.

Every muscle in me goes cold.

Because I know him.

The man beside her.

The name I'd buried under years of therapy and silence.

The drunk driver who killed Gracie.

The screen brightens, oblivious. Monroe's shaking hands with a donor, smiling for the camera, redemption headline crawling across the bottom.

Diesel lifts his head, sensing the change in my breathing.

"It's nothing," I whisper. But my pulse says otherwise.

Outside, the city hums like static. Inside, the air tastes like metal and memory.

For the first time since the crash, I don't know if I'm about to forgive someone—or destroy everything.

Chapter 29 – Sienna

By the time I unlock the rescue door the next morning, Ziggy's already spinning in the middle of the lobby like a glitter tornado.

"We did it!" he shouts. "We broke the internet, Lennon! Broke it, healed it, gave it a dog biscuit!"

"Good morning to you too," I mumble, stepping over three donation boxes stacked by the door.

He clutches a tablet to his chest. "Donations have tripled overnight. People are buying Double Dog Date Ya shirts, mugs, leashes—someone even Venmoed us two grand with the note 'for Diesel's drool fund.'"

Lila appears from the back with a cup of coffee and the same dazed look I probably have. "He's not exaggerating. We're trending on every platform."

"That's amazing," I say. It is—heart-swelling, surreal, a miracle in pixels—but it also makes my stomach flutter with nerves. "What about the interview?"

Ziggy swipes to a replay. The video fills the screen: me laughing, Nate wiping Diesel's slobber off the reporter, everyone doubled over.

"Watch this part," he says, finger tapping the frame. "That right there—when you looked at him? That's the moment America fell in love."

I groan. "Ziggy—"

"Don't 'Ziggy' me, Lennon. The rescue's funded for a year. You're welcome."

Lila nudges me with her elbow. "You've seen the comments, right?"

"I'm trying not to."

She grins. "#SiennaAndNate4Ever. #DroolGoals. #TrueLoveIsMessy."

Ziggy twirls. "I'm ordering shirts."

"Don't you dare."

He's already dialing the printer.

A few hours later, the chaos settles into a rhythm—phones ringing, volunteers laughing, dogs barking like applause. I sneak into the back office, shut the door, and finally let the quiet sink in.

I open my email to find a message from Nate.

Subject: Morning after fame

I think Diesel's demanding an agent. Call me before he signs anything.

I can't help the smile that pulls at my lips. I type back:

Only if you agree to handle his autograph sessions.

His reply comes two minutes later.

Deal. Dinner to discuss contract terms?

I stare at the screen for a long moment, heart doing its ridiculous drum solo.

Maybe it's just dinner.

Maybe it's more.

Maybe it's exactly what I've been afraid to want.

I type one word.

Yes.

A calendar ping slides in above the thread—City Partnership Roundtable – Friday 10:00 a.m. Guest list scrolls past my eyes: vendors, donors… Monroe Adler (community liaison).

My breath catches for a second—old worry brushing a new happiness—then releases. I close the tab.

When I step outside, the afternoon sun is warm and the air smells like fresh coffee from the food truck parked nearby. Volunteers are laughing. The world feels bigger and lighter than it did yesterday.

Ziggy waves from the sidewalk, phone pressed to his ear, already planning something outrageous.

Lila's handing out treats to kids lined up to meet the dogs.

And for the first time in years, I let myself stand still, breathe, and believe.

Love may be messy.

But maybe that's the point.

Chapter 30 – Nate

I haven't been nervous about a dinner since my first job interview.

This feels worse.

I've changed shirts twice. Diesel has circled me every time, tail wagging like a metronome of judgment.

"Don't look at me like that," I tell him. "It's dinner, not destiny."

He tilts his head. I swear the dog smirks.

The restaurant is one of those cozy corner places—brick walls, string lights, the faint hum of jazz. Sienna's already at the table, hair tucked behind one ear, a faint shimmer of nerves she hides behind a smile.

"You made it," she says.

"Would've been rude to leave Diesel's agent waiting."

She laughs, soft and genuine, and suddenly the world shrinks down to the space between us.

A muted TV over the bar idles through local headlines with captions only; a still photo flickers for two seconds— Monroe Adler shaking hands at the park. My jaw tightens, then loosens. Not tonight. I turn back to her.

We order, we talk—about everything except the obvious.

She tells me the rescue's donations hit record numbers.

I tell her Jax's Rottweiler stole my lunch.

She laughs; I pretend not to notice how my chest tightens at the sound.

Between courses, there's a pause. Not awkward—just quiet, comfortable.

"Can I ask you something?" she says.

"Shoot."

"Do you ever stop joking?"

I grin. "Only when I'm asleep."

"I figured." She twirls her straw, eyes thoughtful. "You use humor like armor."

"Better than using silence."

She tilts her head. "What would happen if you put the armor down?"

For a second, I can't answer. The honest one slips out anyway. "I'm afraid everything underneath might fall apart."

Her gaze softens. "Maybe it wouldn't. Maybe it'd finally breathe."

It's such a simple thing, but it hits like truth. I look away before I drown in it.

Our food arrives—pasta for her, steak for me. Diesel's not here, but I still set my napkin across my lap like he's watching.

Halfway through dinner, a kid from another table trips and spills a glass of water right into my lap. The entire restaurant gasps.

Sienna covers her mouth, trying not to laugh.

I look down at the mess, then at her. "Guess true love really is messy."

She loses it—laughing, bright and unguarded. When she finally catches her breath, she hands me a napkin.

"You okay?" she asks, still smiling.

"Better than okay."

After dinner we step outside. The night's cool, the air humming with city noise and possibility.

"Thank you," she says. "For…everything. The events, the chaos, the patience."

"You're thanking me for patience?"

"You've been surprisingly patient."

"Give it time," I say. "I'm new at it."

She laughs again, then quiets. "You know, for a man who claims he doesn't believe in second chances…"

"Yeah?"

"You're pretty good at taking them."

Before I can respond, Diesel—waiting with Jax around the corner—lets out a bark that echoes down the block.

We both laugh. I step closer, close enough to smell lavender and coffee and maybe something like hope.

"It's just dinner," I say.

She meets my eyes, smiling. "Sure. And dogs are just pets."

When she leaves, I stand there watching her go, grinning like an idiot.

Diesel trots up beside me, tail wagging.

"Don't say it," I tell him."

He barks once, triumphant.

"Yeah," I admit, rubbing his head. "I know. We're in trouble."

I glance back through the window. The TV over the bar has rotated to a promo: City Partnership Roundtable – Friday— Monroe's name in the crawl. A small, cold knot returns and sits beside the warmth she left.

Not tonight, I tell myself again.

But tomorrow's coming.

Chapter 31 – Doggy Down Day

A week after the live interview, the city decides to throw itself a sequel.

If you ever want to test the limits of joy and chaos, put forty dogs, twenty hopeful singles, and one Ziggy Daug in a park with free sugar samples.

By noon, Doggy Down Day looks less like a fundraiser and more like a fever dream of barking, laughter, and flirtation.

Ziggy's dressed like Cupid in sunglasses and a pink blazer, directing everyone through a megaphone.

"Remember, my loves—dogs know truth even when humans fake smiles! Hydrate, flirt responsibly, and don't lick anything that isn't yours!"

A golden retriever immediately licks a stranger's face.

The crowd cheers.

Near the entrance, a sponsorship banner flutters in the breeze—City Partnership Program – Monroe Adler, Liaison—but Sienna's too busy chasing runaway volunteers to give the name a second thought.

Ellie & The Dog Walker

At the treat table, Ellie, the rescue's twenty-something social-media intern whose optimism could power the city grid, piles frozen peanut-butter swirls into tiny cones.

Beside her is the new dog walker—tall, tan, perpetually sun-kissed, the kind of man who still owns a skateboard and somehow pulls it off.

She's mid-story when she absent-mindedly grabs his cone instead of hers and takes a heroic lick.

A beat of silence.

He grins. "That one's for dogs."

Ellie freezes. "Oh my God—"

Ziggy appears, camera rolling. "Yes! Love in its rawest, stickiest form!"

The crowd howls. The dog walker hands her a napkin. "Guess that's our first kiss."

Ellie laughs so hard she snorts. Chemistry: confirmed.

Mr. Whittle's Debut

Back by the benches sits Mr. Whittle, the park's unofficial mayor—white hair slicked back, pressed suspenders, a thermos with Marge ♥ etched into the side.

A widower with too much time and endless opinions, he keeps a notebook labeled Observations and dispenses advice like a relationship DJ.

"Hey, kid!" he calls to a man clutching a dachshund. "If the dog likes her, you're already outnumbered!"

To a woman trying to coax her pug into a selfie: "Lower the camera! No one wins from that angle, not even the Pope!"

By mid-afternoon people quote him like scripture.

Ziggy crowns him Saint Whittle of the Leash.

Mr. Whittle tips his hat. "I'm just here for the entertainment—and the free pup-cakes."

Beau & AK

Across the field, Beau and Anna-Katherine—divorced co-parents whose cordial truce has lasted longer than their marriage—find themselves bound together by their kids' puppies.

Avery, nine, and Gunner, ten, are shrieking with laughter as the leashes twist them into a human pretzel.

"Mom, you're blushing!" Avery giggles.

"Dad, you're sweating!" Gunner yells.

AK tugs at the knot. "This is ridiculous."

Beau grins. "Still smoother than our divorce."

She tries not to laugh, fails. "Don't make me like you again."

"Too late."

Mr. Whittle ambles past. "That one'll cost therapy money but end in a hug," he mutters.

Sienna & Nate

Near the donation booth, Sienna checks forms while Nate appears with Diesel, proudly wearing a Volunteer of the Month bandana Ziggy definitely forged.

"Crowd's wild today," Nate says.

"You think?" She ducks a rogue frisbee.

Diesel leaps, catches it mid-air, and drops it at her feet.

"Show-off," she says.

"Runs in the family."

Their eyes meet; laughter softens into that quiet warmth they both pretend not to notice.

From his bench, Mr. Whittle nudges Ziggy. "That's the one, son—you can see it in the posture."

Ziggy fans himself. "Finally, someone who gets it!"

Sunset

By evening, the park glows gold. Dogs nap under picnic tables, people linger over empty plates, and the air hums with that perfect, exhausted kind of happiness that only comes from chaos well survived.

Sienna watches Nate help Ellie pack up the food truck when Mr. Whittle shuffles over.

"Fine day," he says.

"The best," she admits.

He nods. "You know, sweetheart, the trick to finding love isn't looking for it—it's standing still long enough to let it catch up."

Before she can reply, he pats her hand and wanders off to claim another pup-cake.

She looks across the park just in time to see Nate glance over, catch her eye, and smile.

And just like that, she knows—love might really be hiding somewhere in the mess.

She just hopes the mess doesn't get messier.

Chapter 32 – Nate

By the time Diesel and I get home, I'm eighty percent dog hair and twenty percent glitter.

Ziggy's latest post hits my phone before I've unlocked the door.
@ZiggyDaug: *When the heart leads, follow the paw prints.*
Attached: the cone-lick video, Ellie's horrified face in slow motion, me laughing in the background.

I drop my keys on the counter. "He's unstoppable."
Diesel barks once—Ziggy-speak for *likes and shares.*

A shower later, I collapse onto the couch. The TV's on mute—color without sound.
Diesel's curled against my leg, tail thumping in his sleep.

My phone pings again—Ziggy, naturally.
ZIGGY: Trending again! *#TrueLoveIsMessy* just hit three million views!
ME: I'm moving to Canada.
ZIGGY: She laughed at your joke today. Admit it— chemistry.
ME: She laughs at everyone.
ZIGGY: Not like that.

I toss the phone aside, but the truth hums in the room anyway.
Her laugh really did sound different—like the first deep breath after you've been holding one too long.

The next morning at The Yard, Jax has that look—the one that says he's been waiting to pounce.

"Caught the footage," he says, handing me a coffee. "Nice timing with the drool-dodge."

"I didn't dodge. Diesel did."

"Same thing. You planning to keep pretending you're not into her?"

"Into who?"

He just stares. "Man, even your denial's tired."

Tank rumbles a growl that sounds suspiciously like agreement. Diesel, traitor that he is, drops a slobbery tennis ball at Jax's boots.

"Great," I mutter. "Now it's an intervention."

"Listen," Jax says, leaning on the fence. "You've spent half your life outrunning ghosts. Maybe this one finally caught you."

I stare into my coffee. Diesel's tail thumps dust into the sunlight.

"Maybe," I say.

"Good. Because you're grinning like a man who's already lost the argument."

Back at the apartment, I scroll through Ziggy's feed again. The newest post isn't a video—it's a photo. Sienna stands in the middle of the park at sunset, Diesel asleep at her feet, eyes lifted toward something out of frame. Me, probably.

Caption: *Sometimes the dogs pick right.*

I try to be annoyed. I really do. But the smile gets there first.

"Fine," I tell Diesel, scratching his ear. "Maybe she laughs at me a little differently."
He licks my hand, smug as ever.

That night I text her.
ME: So, remind me what chaos you're planning next.
SIENNA: Thinking fundraiser gala—no dogs, fewer cones.
ME: Boring.
SIENNA: You'd miss the mess.
ME: Probably.

When the typing dots vanish, I lean back. Outside, the city glows like someone left the lights on for us.

For the first time, I stop trying to imagine how this ends. I just let it start.

A single news alert scrolls across the muted TV: "City Partnership Program – Monroe Adler expands outreach." I ignore it—for now.

Chapter 33 – Sienna

If love is messy, a charity gala is its formalwear cousin—
still chaos, just in heels.

The rescue office looks like a craft-store explosion.
Ziggy crouches on the floor surrounded by ribbon, glitter,
and what might once have been a glue gun.

"Ziggy," I ask carefully, "what is that?"
He looks up, eyes wild. "Art. Possibly a centerpiece.
Possibly a fire hazard."

Lila leans against the doorframe, coffee in hand. "We're
going to need more candles and fewer creative impulses."
"I heard that," Ziggy says. "And I reject it."

I set my clipboard on the desk. "Focus. Venue?"
"Confirmed," Lila says. "Community hall by the park."
"Catering?"
"Food-truck couple. They're calling it the Pup-Gala
Menu—lots of bark-scotti."
"Perfect."

Ziggy twirls a ribbon. "And our theme is—wait for it—
Love, Unleashed! Or maybe *Paws for the Cause.* Still
workshopping."
Lila mutters, "Lord help us."

A knock saves me. Mr. Whittle—the park's unofficial
mayor, pressed suspenders, thermos etched *Marge* ♥—
pokes his head in, hat in hand.
"Morning, ladies. Brought the volunteers donuts. And
gossip."

"Both welcome," I say.

He strolls in, setting the box on the desk. "Saw our young Mr. Callahan this morning. He was buying flowers. Big ones."

Ziggy gasps so loudly a donut falls off the box. "For who?"

Mr. Whittle grins. "Didn't ask. Didn't have to."

Heat crawls up my neck. "He's probably thanking a donor."

"Sure," he says. "Or maybe he's remembering my advice."

"What advice was that?" Lila asks.

" 'If the dog likes her, he's already outnumbered,' " he recites proudly.

Ziggy fans himself. "The prophecy!"

"Enough," I say, laughing despite myself. "We have a gala to plan."

Mr. Whittle winks. "Don't worry, sweetheart. Whatever it is you're building here—it's already working."

That afternoon the rescue buzzes: volunteers stringing lights, painting signs, Diesel supervising from a blanket. I'm bent over the seating chart when my phone buzzes.

NATE: Do I need a tux for this thing, or will sarcasm be acceptable attire?

ME: Black tie, minimum. Diesel's wearing a bowtie.

NATE: Of course he is. I'll try to live up to his standard.

ME: Impossible.

NATE: That's what you like about me.

I shake my head, smiling.

Ziggy appears like a magician. "Was that your not-boyfriend? Tell him to bring the flowers he bought this morning."

"How do you—"
He taps his temple. "Empathic Wi-Fi."
"Ziggy."
"What? I ship it."

When everyone leaves, I walk the hall, checking strings of lights. The room smells like paint, sugar, and anticipation. It feels like something's about to happen—something big.

I pause in the doorway, watching Diesel nap beside Mr. Whittle's chair while he hums to himself.
"Big night coming," he says without looking up.
"Yeah," I whisper. "It really is."

A volunteer calls from the foyer—asking where to hang the new sponsor banner. I catch the words "City Partnership Program" and "Monroe Adler." The name flickers across my mind and disappears into the hum of string lights.

Chapter 34 – Nate

Two weeks after the TV chaos and one nerve-wrecking city meeting later, the gala arrives.

I've faced boardrooms, bad markets, and one very aggressive raccoon that got into my garbage last year.

Nothing compares to this.

The community hall glitters—literally. Ziggy's gone nuclear with fairy lights. Banners shout LOVE UNLEASHED! and Paws for the Cause because apparently we're incapable of choosing one slogan.

Diesel's wearing a bow tie.

I'm in a tux.

We're both uncomfortable.

"Don't even think about it," I tell him as he eyes the buffet. "You throw up at this thing and we're banned from society."

He yawns. Traitor.

Ziggy flutters by with a headset like he's directing the Oscars.

"Darling!" he says, sweeping up to me. "You clean up nicely. Channeling 'reluctant James Bond.'"

"I'm just here for the free champagne."

He presses a glass into my hand. "Then drink and sparkle. We have donors to charm, dogs to pet, hearts to open."

"I think you've got that last part covered."

He grins. "Oh no, sweetheart. Tonight, that's your department."

Monroe's name is still plastered across the partnership banner outside. I tell myself I'm here for Sienna, not ghosts.

And then she walks in.

Sienna.

Hair swept up, simple blue dress that catches the light, eyes holding it hostage.

She laughs at something Mr. Whittle says, smooths Diesel's bow tie as she passes.

Everything else blurs.

Ziggy follows my gaze, sighs like a proud parent. "And there it is. Cue the orchestra."

"Don't start."

"Too late."

The night spins fast—handshakes, speeches, applause—but every few minutes, my eyes find her.

When it's her turn to speak, she steps to the mic, calm and bright.

"Tonight's about love in every form—messy, loud, unconditional. Our dogs remind us what forgiveness looks like. Thank you for helping us rescue that kind of love."

Applause swells.

Ziggy's dabbing his eyes with a napkin.

Even Diesel barks once, approving.

When she steps offstage, I'm waiting.

"You did great," I say.

"You heard all that over Ziggy's sniffles?"

"Barely."

She smiles, a little shy. "Thank you for coming."

"I wouldn't miss it."

For a heartbeat we just stand there—music pulsing, lights spinning.

Then the band starts something slow and old, and Ziggy materializes again, whispering, "Dance floor, lovers. Don't make me drag you."

Sienna laughs. "You heard the man."

We move to the floor.

Her hand fits in mine like it's been rehearsed.

We're not graceful—she keeps stepping on my shoe, I keep pretending not to notice—but it doesn't matter.

"Diesel's judging us," I say quietly.

"Let him."

"Pretty sure he thinks I'm falling for you."

She tilts her head. "Pretty sure you are."

Caught. No defense left.

"Yeah," I admit. "I think I am."

She looks up, smiling, eyes soft and steady. "Good."

When the song ends, we don't let go right away.

Ziggy cheers from across the room.

Mr. Whittle raises his glass and shouts, "About time!"

Everyone claps, whistles.

Diesel barks, tail thumping in rhythm.

For once, I don't mind being in the spotlight.

Later, after the crowd thins, I find her on the balcony overlooking the park, the night air cool and full of city hum.

"I didn't thank you properly," she says.

"For what?"

"For letting yourself show up."

I brush a strand of hair from her face. "That's all it took, huh? Showing up?"

She nods. "That's where everything starts."

I smile. "Then here's to starting."

She leans in, close enough that the world goes quiet.

Then Diesel sneezes so loudly it echoes.

We break into laughter, forehead to forehead.

"Always the chaperone," she whispers.

"Always," I say, still laughing. "Guess we're stuck with him."

"Good," she says. "I like his taste."

Chapter 35 – Sienna

Morning sunlight filters through the rescue's front windows, scattering across the floor in stripes of gold and dust.

The place smells like lavender cleaner, cinnamon pup-treats, and something new: hope.

Ziggy lies flat on his back in the lobby, surrounded by empty coffee cups and a mountain of donation envelopes.

Lila crouches beside him, sorting checks into neat stacks.

"Good morning, survivors," I say.

Ziggy sits up, hair sticking out in every direction. "We raised twenty-five thousand dollars," he croaks. "I have glitter in places no sage can cleanse."

Lila grins. "You were magnificent. Even Mr. Whittle said you're the loudest miracle he's ever seen."

"That's because I am a miracle." Ziggy staggers upright, clutching his heart. "But Lennon—last night? That was you. The way he looked at you? Honey, even the band stopped playing for a second."

"Ziggy—"

"Don't 'Ziggy' me," he says, pointing at me with a donation envelope. "That was capital-L Love and you know it."

Lila slides another stack of checks across the table. "She's right, you know. And these numbers prove the universe agrees."

I roll my eyes, but my cheeks won't stop warming.

It's ridiculous, the way one smile can replay like a favorite song.

By noon, the rescue hums again. Volunteers sweep up streamers; dogs chase leftover balloons.

Mr. Whittle—the park's unofficial mayor—sits on his bench, coffee in hand, holding court for a gaggle of teenagers.

He waves when he sees me. "Morning, sweetheart. I caught the broadcast replay."

"Oh no."

"Oh yes." His grin is pure mischief. "If I were twenty years younger, I'd enter myself in that contest."

I laugh. "You'd win."

"Course I would. But I'd lose to that boy of yours."

"He's not—" I stop, because arguing feels pointless. "Thank you, Mr. Whittle."

He tips his hat. "Just remember: people can fake a lot of things, but dogs don't bless every hand they meet."

When I step inside, Diesel barrels toward me, skidding across the floor until he stops at my feet.

He sits, tail sweeping, and looks up expectantly.

"Where is he?" I ask.

Ziggy pops his head out of the office. "He dropped Diesel off an hour ago. Said he had meetings."

Meetings. Sure.

Diesel whines softly and nudges my knee.

"Yeah," I whisper, scratching behind his ears. "I miss him too."

That evening, I walk through the park.

The fairy lights from last night still hang between the trees, faintly glowing.

A few volunteers are taking them down, laughing quietly.

I sit on the same bench where Mr. Whittle always sits, watching the sunset paint the sky in amber.

My phone buzzes.

NATE: The city's quiet without barking. You okay?

ME: Exhausted. Happy. You?

NATE: Trying to remember what normal feels like.

ME: Maybe this is normal now.

NATE: If it is, I'm in.

I smile, tuck the phone away. The last light dips behind the buildings, and Diesel's soft bark echoes from somewhere down the path.

For the first time in years, the future doesn't scare me.

It smells like lavender, sounds like laughter, and feels a lot like a second chance.

Chapter 36—Nate

Meetings. That's what I told her, anyway.

Technically true—just not the kind that involve spreadsheets.

Jax sits across from me at The Yard, Tank snoring between us. Diesel sprawls near the gate, drooling on my shoe.

"You really think this will work?" Jax asks.

"It's not a plan," I say. "It's logistics."

"Logistics that involve fairy lights, catering, and Ziggy ordering a confetti cannon."

"Exactly."

Jax chuckles. "You're doomed."

Ziggy bursts through the gate, glittered folder in hand. "Operation Second Chance is a GO!"

"Why does it have a name?" I ask.

"Because branding matters! This—my emotionally constipated friend—is how we make Sienna Lennon's dreams permanent."

He spreads a hand-drawn park map across the table: new kennels, shaded training area, community garden. At the top: The Lennon Rescue Center.

"She's going to kill me," I say.

"She's going to kiss you," Ziggy corrects. "Trust the process."

Jax whistles low. "You already have the donations?"

"Between the gala, sponsors, and my checkbook—yeah."

Jax grins. "Not bad for a guy who thought love was a bad investment."

"Still might be."

Ziggy pats my shoulder. "Darling, that's called yield."

Later, I walk the park with Diesel. The fairy lights from the last event still hang. Mr. Whittle's on his bench, thermos in hand.

"Evening, son," he says. "You look like a man about to jump off a cliff."

"Feels about right."

"Good. That's how you know it's worth it."

We sit a while, watching Diesel chase shadows.

"You ever plan something for someone and worry it's too much?" I ask.

"If it's for the right person," he says, "it's never too much. It's just right on time."

Diesel barks once—agreement.

I hit send on the email to the city office: Proposal for Lennon Rescue Center Expansion.

The confirmation pings back, and for the first time, commitment feels like home.

Chapter 37—Sienna

Mondays are supposed to be quiet.

Coffee, paperwork, a little background barking—simple.

Instead, I walk into the rescue and find Ziggy pacing like a man guarding state secrets.

Lila's perched on the counter with her coffee, grinning.

"What's going on?" I ask.

Ziggy thrusts a tablet at me. "You might want to sit."

It's an email chain: Proposal for Lennon Rescue Center Expansion.

My name, bold in the header.

"He's funding… everything?"

Ziggy clasps his hands. "The Lennon Rescue Center. It's happening."

I just stare. Lila steadies me. "You okay?"

"I don't know how to process someone doing something that kind."

Ziggy wipes an imaginary tear. "This is what happens when emotionally unavailable men fall for women with purpose. They build temples."

"Ziggy."

"What? It's romantic!"

"Good," I say, half laughing, half crying. "He should be nervous."

Later, at the park, Nate's waiting by the fountain, Diesel at his feet.

"Hey," I say.

"Hey."

I hold up the tablet. "So. The Lennon Rescue Center?"

He winces. "Surprise?"

"Ziggy almost had a cardiac event."

"Then it worked."

"You didn't have to do this."

"I wanted to."

"Why?"

He meets my eyes. "Because you save everything you touch, and it was time somebody built something for you."

Tears sting. "You're ridiculous. And wonderful."

"Start with dinner," he says. "This time I'll try not to get baptized in sparkling water."

I laugh. "Deal."

That evening, the three of us stand in the park. The lights glow, the fountain hums, and for the first time, everything feels perfectly, beautifully quiet.

Chapter 38— Sienna

Hospitals always smell the same—sterile air over something faintly metallic, like fear with a fresh coat of paint.

Fluorescent lights hum overhead; everything feels too white, too quiet.

He's in the supply room, folding towels. Older. Thinner. A tremor in his hands.

"Sienna," he says. "You came."

I see the boy who used to sneak me candy—and the man who vanished the night my mother died.

"Why now?"

"Because I finally remember all of it. And because I need you to know the truth."

"I didn't sell to her," he says. "I introduced her to someone who did. I thought I could control it. I told myself I was protecting her."

"You knew she was using."

He nods. "I thought if I was part of it, I could save her. But I just made it easier."

"You destroyed us."

"I know. And I live with it every day. I don't expect forgiveness. I just couldn't die without you knowing."

The flashback crashes in—antiseptic, gurney wheels, her hand slipping out of mine.

Her last words: Don't let them take Monroe to jail.

"I don't know if I can forgive you," I whisper. "But I can't hate you anymore either."

He covers his face. "That's more than I deserve."

I touch his arm. "I hope you keep building things that matter."

"I will."

When I leave, the air feels different—lighter, like rain finally breaking.

Chapter 39—Nate

The hallway smells like antiseptic and rain on old tile.

Sienna's footsteps fade toward the exit—quick, uneven—and I stay behind, staring through the small window at Monroe.

He sits on the edge of his cot, head bowed, hands clasped like a man trying to remember how to pray.

Diesel leans against my leg, ears flicking.

"Easy, boy," I whisper. "He's already been punished enough."

I push the door open. Monroe flinches, then looks up, recognition dawning. "You're with her."

"Yeah. But this isn't about her right now."

He nods, eyes rimmed red. "She shouldn't have come back. I don't deserve it."

"Maybe not," I say. "But you got it anyway."

I cross the room and rest a hand on his shoulder. He tenses, then exhales—like letting go costs him something.

"She's okay," I tell him. "Stronger than either of us thought."

He nods, tears cutting clean paths down his face. "Thank you."

I squeeze once and step back. Diesel's waiting by the door, tail sweeping the floor.

"Come on, partner," I murmur. "We've got her now."

Jax finds me at The Yard that evening.

He looks the same as always—tall, sweat-damp T-shirt clinging to his chest, streaks of dirt on his jaw, every inch of him built from work and quiet conviction.

He hands me a beer without a word and leans against the fence beside me. We stand there a while, watching Diesel and Tank chase the last light of day.

"You're brooding," he says finally.

"Always am."

"Brooding's only useful if you learn something from it."

I take a drink. "You moonlight as a philosopher now?"

He chuckles, low and rough. "Nah. Just a guy who's seen too many people think they can outrun their ghosts."

I tell him everything—Monroe, the hospital, the apology. Saying it out loud makes the air feel lighter.

"You going to her?" he asks.

"I don't know what to say."

"Then don't," he says. "Just show up. That's the only thing that ever works."

He straightens, stretches, the motion easy and strong. "You'll figure it out. You're not your old man."

The words land harder than he means them to. I nod once, grateful and unsettled all at once.

"See you at dawn?" he asks.

"Do I have a choice?"

"Never."

He grins, whistles for Tank, and they disappear into the twilight like a myth I'm still learning to believe in.

When I find Sienna later, she's sitting by the fountain.

The water throws gold light across her face; Diesel noses ahead, tail wagging.

She looks up and smiles, tired but real.

"Hey," I say.

"Hey." Her voice is soft. "You didn't have to come."

"I did."

I sit beside her. The space between us hums with everything said and unsaid.

"How's Monroe?"

"Trying," she says. "For once, that's enough."

"I should've told you I knew him," I admit. "We weren't close, but I should've said it."

"I get it. You thought it would hurt me."

"I thought you'd see the worst parts of me and think that's all that was left."

"I saw them," she says. "But I also saw you in that hallway—standing outside that room like you were guarding the whole building. That's who you are now."

Diesel rests his head on her knee, tail thumping once.

"Your dog always knows when forgiveness shows up."

"He's got better instincts than I do."

"Maybe not anymore."

"You sure you're okay?"

"I'm getting there."

"Good," I say. "Because I'm not leaving your side."

She leans against me, head under my chin. "Promise?"

"Yeah."

I wrap an arm around her shoulders. "You've carried enough alone."

She exhales, the sound catching in her throat. "Feels lighter now."

Diesel sighs between us, tail flicking lazily in approval.

For a long time, we sit there—three survivors of three different storms, finally still.

Chapter 40—The Fallout

The next morning, Sienna's at the rescue early, sleeves rolled, pretending she still has something left to scrub.

Diesel shadows her every move, nails clicking on the tile.

Ziggy bursts through the doorway, incense in one hand and a latte in the other.

"Emergency vibe calibration!" he announces. "Grief leaves residue."

"Ziggy, please—"

He waves her off. "Don't argue with sage, Lennon."

Before she can answer, Nate walks in. He takes the clipboard from her hands and sets it aside.

"Stop working for five minutes," he says quietly.

"I'm fine."

"You're shaking."

She opens her mouth to argue, but he's already pulled her into his arms.

It isn't romance yet—it's refuge. His shirt smells like coffee and rain.

"He doesn't get to hurt you anymore," he murmurs against her hair.

Ziggy peeks from behind a kennel door, stage-whispers to Lila, "That's the best energy clearing I've ever seen."

Lila elbows him. "Let them have their moment."

Sienna presses her face against Nate's chest, breathing him in until her heartbeat evens out.

"I'm okay," she says finally.

He leans back just enough to look at her. "Yeah," he says. "Now you are."

Mr. Whittle ambles in, coffee in hand. He watches a moment before saying, "Sometimes what you need isn't a fix. It's a wall to lean on till the wind dies down."

Nate glances up. "Guess I'm the wall."

"Guess you are," Mr. Whittle says, smiling.

Diesel huffs once, settles at their feet, and the whole rescue seems to exhale with him.

Chapter 41—Forgiveness

Two days later, sunlight spills through hospital windows, soft and clean.

Sienna goes back to see Monroe. Nate waits in the hallway.

Inside, Monroe's sitting by the window, sunlight across his face.

"I'm not angry anymore," she says.

"I'm working here full-time," he answers quietly. "It helps."

"You always mattered," she tells him. "You just got lost."

He shakes his head. "I don't deserve that."

"No one ever does," she says. "That's why it's called forgiveness."

When she leaves, Nate's there. She walks straight into him.

"It's done," she whispers.

"Good," he says. "Then we can start living again."

Mr. Whittle's voice drifts down the hall. "Real love's not rescuing each other. It's guarding what you built after the storm."

Nate smiles. "Then yeah. I'm guarding it."

That night, peace settles slowly—scent by scent, heartbeat by heartbeat.

BRIDGE SCENE — LAVENDER BETWEEN STORMS

The park is almost empty when Sienna leaves the hospital.

Rain has just stopped, leaving everything damp and shining—sidewalks, benches, the lavender patch by the rescue entrance.

The scent rises with the steam off the ground: clean, alive, and faintly sweet.

She kneels by the flowers, presses her palms to the wet earth. It's cool under her hands, grounding. Her chest still feels raw, but there's air there now—space where anger used to live.

For the first time in years, she doesn't picture her mother on the stretcher. She just hears her voice—softer, steadier: Don't let them take him to jail.

Maybe it was never a plea for justice. Maybe it was a plea for mercy.

Behind her, Diesel's nails click across the walkway. He sits close, leaning his head against her shoulder until she laughs—quiet and surprised.

"Hey, boy." Her voice is hoarse. "You found me."

He yawns, as if to say of course.

She takes a deep breath, letting the lavender fill her lungs. The scent clings to her skin and his fur.

"Smells like peace," she whispers.

Footsteps approach. She doesn't turn, but she knows it's Nate—the air changes when he's near.

He stops behind her, close enough that she can hear him breathe.

"You okay?" he asks quietly.

"I will be," she says. "It's strange. Forgiveness doesn't feel like forgetting. It feels like finally setting something down."

He nods. "Then let it stay down. I'll carry the rest with you."

She looks up at him, lavender shimmering between them, and for once there's nothing left to hide behind.

Diesel noses her hand into Nate's, a gentle command.

They both laugh—that new kind of laugh, the one that doesn't hurt.

Sienna squeezes Nate's hand. "Let's go home."

As they walk away, the lavender sways in the breeze— roots deep, petals trembling—peace growing exactly where pain used to live.

Chapter 42 – Nate

It takes me three tries to walk through the hospital doors.

Not because I'm scared of Monroe — because I'm terrified of saying something that might break Sienna's peace.

He's in the volunteer lounge, folding towels. Older, thinner, a steadiness in his hands that wasn't there before.

When he looks up, there's no surprise — just quiet acceptance, like he's been waiting for this.

"Callahan," he says.

"Monroe."

We stand there in a silence thick enough to cut. Diesel sits beside me, head high, reading the tension like radar.

"I figured this was coming," Monroe says finally.

"Good. Saves time." I step closer. "You hurt her."

"I know."

"She forgave you."

"I still know."

"Then make it worth something."

He meets my eyes. "That's the plan."

"She's stronger than anyone I've ever met," I tell him. "But strong doesn't mean unbreakable.

You ever drag her back into that pain again, I don't care how many therapy groups you lead — I'll make sure you regret it."

He doesn't flinch. "You love her?"

"Yeah," I say simply. "I do."

He exhales. "Good. Then you'll take better care of her than I ever did."

Diesel nudges his hand. Monroe scratches behind his ears, tentative.

"He still remembers me, huh?"

"He remembers everything that matters," I say. "Same as she does."

I turn to go, but Monroe calls after me. "For what it's worth, I'm glad she found you."

"Me too," I admit, and leave it at that.

Outside, the sun's low and the city hums like it's breathing again.

Diesel trots ahead, tail wagging, and for once the world feels balanced.

Maybe peace doesn't mean still.

Maybe it just means together.

Chapter 43 – Coming Home

When Diesel goes missing, my heart stops for exactly forty-seven seconds.

One minute he's asleep at my feet while I update donor spreadsheets; the next, the front door's cracked open and he's gone.

"Ziggy!" I shout.

He pops up from behind the desk clutching a sage stick. "He's probably just manifesting adventure!"

"Manifest him back!"

We tear through the park calling his name until Lila spots paw prints leading toward The Yard.

Nate's already there when I arrive — because of course he is.

Diesel sits proudly in the middle of the training field, tail thumping, tongue lolling like he's proud of himself.

"He showed up ten minutes ago," Nate says, walking toward me. "Ran straight through the gate like he owned the place."

I drop to my knees and wrap my arms around Diesel's neck. "You scared me half to death."

He whines softly, licking my chin.

"He just wanted a reunion," Jax says from the fence. "Guy's got better timing than Ziggy's megaphone."

Ziggy appears, winded. "The universe led him here for closure! I felt it!"

I look up at Nate, exasperated and relieved all at once. "You sent him psychic directions, didn't you?"

He smiles. "Maybe he just knows where home is."

The word home hangs there — warm, dangerous, true. We both feel it.

I stand, brushing grass from my knees. "You could've called, you know."

"I was waiting for you to come find me," he says. "Worked, didn't it?"

I shake my head, smiling despite myself. "You're impossible."

"Everyone keeps saying that," he says, stepping closer. "But nobody leaves."

Before I can reply, Diesel shoves his head between us, tail wagging like a referee demanding a tie.

Nate laughs. "Fine, we'll call it even."

Jax claps once. "Alright, therapy session's over. Let's get this dog a treat before he starts scheduling his own events."

Ziggy gasps. "Brilliant idea! Double Dog Date Ya: The Reunion Tour!"

"Ziggy, no," we all say at once.

He sighs dramatically. "Killjoys, the lot of you."

The next morning, the rescue smells like coffee, paint, and possibility.

Lila's perched on my desk surrounded by receipts and empty muffin wrappers.

I'm pretending to inventory donations — pretending I'm not glowing.

"Stop pretending to work," she says.

"I'm not —"

"You are. And you're smiling. Big. Like a woman whose heart finally unclenched."

I exhale. "It's weird. I feel happy. Actually happy. And that's… terrifying."

She leans back in her chair. "You've been bracing for impact your whole life. Maybe it's okay to land."

"I'm not used to stillness."

"Then learn it," she says gently. "You deserve quiet that doesn't hurt."

"I forgave him, Lila. Monroe. I really did."

She nods. "Of course you did. You've been teaching everyone else how to heal — you just forgot to include yourself."

Before I can respond, Diesel bounds into the office, tail sweeping a pile of papers onto the floor.

Nate's behind him, coffee and pup-cakes in hand.

"Morning," he says, grinning. "I brought bribes."

Lila takes one coffee and heads for the door. "My cue to leave. Lovebirds need caffeine, not witnesses."

As she passes, she adds softly, "Remember what I said — quiet can be good."

Nate sets a cup in front of me. "She's right, you know."

"I hate how everyone keeps saying that."

He laughs. "Get used to it."

Diesel flops under the desk, sighing like he's finally satisfied with how the universe turned out.

Saturday morning, the park glows gold and green.

Beau's truck pulls up just as we finish setting up tables for the volunteer day.

His kids, Gunner and Avery, spill out arguing about who forgot the dog treats.

Anna-Katherine follows, leash in one hand, coffee in the other, looking like she hasn't decided whether to laugh or scold.

"Morning," I call.

"Hey, Lennon," Beau says. "Kids wanted to see Diesel again."

AK grins. "Let's be honest — the kids wanted to see Nate's dog."

Diesel barks once, clearly agreeing.

They all join in helping without being asked — filling water bowls, tying balloons.

It's chaotic and comfortable, the kind of noise that sounds like life.

After a while, the kids chase the puppies toward the fountain, leaving Beau and AK standing side by side with that half-smile you only see between people who know too much about each other.

"You two okay?" I ask.

Beau glances at her, then back at me. "Better than we've been in years."

AK laughs softly. "We remembered we actually like each other — just not living in the same house."

"Co-parenting looks good on you," I say.

Beau nods. "She's the better half of this operation anyway."

AK rolls her eyes, smiling. "He finally admits it."

Mr. Whittle strolls past with his coffee, chuckling. "That's love, kids. Not the fireworks — just the peace after."

Beau laughs. "Guess we're finally there."

They both look out toward their children, doubled over laughing as Diesel splashes through the fountain with them.

And for the first time in a long time, it feels like the world has caught its breath.

As the sun sinks, volunteers pack up tables, and laughter trails into evening.

Ziggy is still arguing with the food-truck couple about branding opportunities, and Mr. Whittle is pretending not to nap on his bench.

Nate slides his hand into mine, Diesel's leash looped around his other wrist.

"This is what she built," he murmurs.

I squeeze his hand. "What we built."

He smiles, eyes soft. "Then I guess we'd better take good care of it."

Diesel nudges our legs, tail sweeping slow and steady — like a heartbeat finally finding its rhythm.

Chapter 44 – Ellie & the Dog Walker 2.0

The park smells like sugar, grass, and second chances.

Ellie wipes down the food-truck counter while the late-afternoon crowd drifts between tables.

Her golden retriever, Sundae, lounges under the window, tongue out, tail flicking lazily against the pavement.

Riley—the new dog walker—leans against the truck, leash looped around his wrist, grin too bright for anyone's emotional safety.

"So," he says, "I've been thinking about our first date."

Ellie squints. "The one where I licked your dog's ice cream?"

"Exactly. Can't top that, so I figured we'd reenact it."

She laughs, shaking her head. "You're never letting that go, are you?"

"Not when it made you laugh like that."

She tosses him a napkin. "Fine. New rule: I pick the dessert this time."

"Deal." He holds up two cones—one chocolate, one peanut-butter swirl. "And these are definitely the human kind."

She arches a brow. "You're sure?"

"Positive," he says, handing one over with mock solemnity.

She takes a careful lick. "Safe so far."

Sundae jumps up, nudging her elbow. Chocolate smears across her cheek, and Riley bursts out laughing.

"Real smooth," she says, grabbing a napkin.

"Hey, it's tradition." He wipes the smear from her cheek with his thumb before he realizes what he's doing.

They freeze for half a second.

"Sorry," he says quietly.

"Don't be," she murmurs, still smiling. "Guess we're even now."

Mr. Whittle strolls past with his thermos. "Back in my day, we just shared milkshakes," he says. "Less dog spit, same result."

Ellie laughs. Riley winks. Sundae barks once, delighted.

Later, when the park lights flicker on, they sit side by side on the tailgate of Riley's truck, Sundae snoring between them.

He tells her about the rescue dogs he walks; she tells him how Ziggy convinced her to join Double Dog Date Ya.

"So technically," Riley says, "we owe the universe."

"Or Ziggy."

"Same thing."

She laughs, looking at him over the dog. "Think the universe plans third dates?"

He bumps her shoulder. "Pretty sure the dog already RSVP'd."

Ellie rests her head against his arm. "Good. I'm tired of being the punch line of the cone story."

"Then we'll make a new one," he says.

Between their laughter and the lavender-scented breeze drifting from the garden, the world feels like it's starting over.

Chapter 45 – The Widow & the Mechanic

The mechanic's name is Tom Alvarez, and everyone knows his shop by the smell of motor oil and cinnamon gum.

Today, though, the park smells different—fresh paint, dog shampoo, and a trace of lavender from the rescue's new garden.

Margaret, the widow with the soft gray eyes, stands beside him under the oak tree.

Her terrier, Daisy, yaps at the bulldog lounging near Tom's boots.

"She's saying hi," Margaret says.

"She's saying, 'that's my man,' " Tom chuckles, scratching the bulldog's head.

"Vet says he's in remission. I can finally stop sleeping on the floor next to his bed."

Margaret's eyes glisten. "That's wonderful. I prayed for him every night."

Tom smiles, small and real. "Guess it worked."

Silence settles—comfortable, easy. The kind of quiet you want to keep.

"I never thought I'd get used to talking about the future again," she admits.

"You don't have to get used to it alone."

She looks up, smiling. "Coffee tomorrow?"

"Always."

Mr. Whittle passes with a donut, tipping his hat. "Told you dogs were the best matchmakers on the planet."

They laugh, and the bulldog's tail thumps once in agreement.

Chapter 46 – Ziggy & Benji

The vet clinic smells like eucalyptus and antiseptic—
Benji's version of calm.

Ziggy bursts through the door carrying two cups of chai
and enough energy to power the lights.

"Morning, Doctor Dreamboat!"

Benji glances up from a chart. "You're five hours early."

"The universe told me punctuality is sexy."

"The universe also told me you'd forget the cream."

Ziggy freezes. "Did I?"

Benji grins. "No. I just like watching you panic."

Their laughter ricochets off white tile like sunlight.

"I, uh, came to ask if you'd co-host a wellness day at the
rescue," Ziggy blurts.

"Free check-ups, adoption cuddles—purely professional."

Benji wipes a streak of glitter from Ziggy's cheek. "You mean an excuse to see me again."

"I'm multi-dimensional," Ziggy insists.

"Ridiculously so," Benji says.

"Ridiculously charming?"

"Ridiculously mine."

He kisses him before he can speak.

Outside, Mr. Whittle taps the window with his coffee cup and mouths, About time, before strolling away.

Chapter 47 – Nate & Monroe

The community garden hums with bees and soft conversation.

Monroe kneels in the soil, planting seedlings. Diesel sniffs every row like a foreman.

"She says you're volunteering full-time," I tell him.

"Feels right. Building instead of breaking."

We work quietly for a while, the sound of children's laughter drifting from the playground.

"She forgave you," I say.

He nods. "Still working on forgiving myself."

"You will. Takes time."

He glances over. "You too?"

"Yeah. My old man, mostly. Myself, a little."

I pat the soil. "Love's just maintenance—you keep showing up."

He smiles. "Thanks for looking out for her."

"Always," I say—and mean it.

Chapter 48 – Forgiveness Gala

Dusk turns the park lavender.

A new sign glints in the lights: THE LENNON RESCUE CENTER.

People gather—volunteers, donors, every couple who found love in the chaos.

Ziggy and Benji hand out heart-and-paw cookies.

Lila corrals puppies.

Mr. Whittle raises his thermos in salute.

Sienna steps to the mic.

"This started as a dare," she says, voice steady. "A messy, ridiculous dare that showed us joy can grow anywhere—if we let it.

These dogs taught us to forgive, to laugh, to stay.

This garden"—she gestures toward the lavender—"is for them, and for everyone still learning that peace doesn't mean perfect.

It means home."

She passes the mic to me. I shake my head. "You said it all."

Diesel barks once. Laughter ripples through the crowd.

Music swells. Sienna pulls me onto the dance floor under the lights.

Mr. Whittle leans toward Ziggy. "If that's not love, I'll eat my hat."

"Please don't," Ziggy whispers. "It's vintage."

Lavender drifts on the wind—the scent of peace and second chances.

Chapter 49 – Gala Finale

The park glows under fairy lights.

Couples dance; dogs nap at their feet.

Beau and Anna-Katherine laugh with their kids by the fountain.

Ellie and Riley share a pup-cake.

Margaret and Tom sway near the bandstand.

Ziggy twirls Benji dramatically until they both collapse in laughter.

Sienna slips her hand into mine. "Look what we built."

I grin. "Look what you built."

She shakes her head. "We did this together."

I pull her closer. "Then we'd better take good care of it."

Diesel circles us once, sighs, and flops down at our feet.

Somewhere behind us, Mr. Whittle chuckles. "Told you the dog always knows before the people do."

Sienna smiles up at me. "Maybe peace isn't quiet after all."

"Maybe it's laughter," I say. "And lavender."

We dance until the music fades and the stars take over.

Epilogue

Morning sunlight spills across the new sign: THE LENNON & CALLAHAN RESCUE CENTER.

Children plant lavender along the walkway while volunteers hang new leashes on the wall.

Ziggy films a promo, shouting, "Welcome to year two of Double Dog Date Ya! Where love is messy and the dogs run the show!"

Benji steals his mic. "And vaccinations are half-off!"

Sienna steps out with her coffee; I follow, Diesel padding between us.

"Still smells like home," I say.

"Always will."

Diesel rolls into the lavender, scattering petals everywhere.

Sienna laughs. "Love's still messy."

"Yeah," I say, kissing her forehead. "But I double-dog dare you to find anything better."

Lavender waves in the morning breeze—the scent of peace, rooted deep.

To the Readers:

Thank you for spending time with Nate, Sienna, and the
dogs who

remind us that love is always a little messy—but always
worth it.

If this story made you smile, laugh, or believe in second
chances,

please consider leaving a short review. Your words help
more

readers discover the stories that feel like home.

To connect with us or share your thoughts,

email us at ForgedInFireStudios@gmail.com

From my heart to yours—thank you for reading.

About the Author

Stephanie Green is a storyteller, dreamer, and the creative heart behind Forged in Fire Studios.

Her work celebrates love, second chances, and the beautiful mess of being human—often with a dog or two at the center of it all.

When she's not writing, Stephanie can be found creating art, designing recovery-inspired projects, or spending time with her husband Jamie and their three kids—Jaylen, Ava, and CJ—plus the family's two beloved dogs, Sugar and Nicky.

She believes that hope can be found in every comeback, laughter is its own kind of healing, and that sometimes the dogs really do know best.

To connect or share your thoughts, email:

ForgedInFireStudios@gmail.com

Made in the USA
Middletown, DE
08 December 2025

21912646R00141